AN HISTORICAL NOVEL BY
DAVID FITZ-GERALD

WANDERS FAR

AN UNLIKELY HERO'S JOURNEY
PART OF THE ADIRONDACK SPIRIT SERIES

outskirts
press

Wanders Far-An Unlikely Hero's Journey
Part of the Adirondack Spirit Series
All Rights Reserved.
Copyright © 2019 David Fitz-Gerald
v4.0

This is a work of fiction. Names, characters, businesses, places, events, locales, and incidents are either the products of the author's imagination or used in a fictitious manner. Any resemblance to actual persons, living or dead, or actual events is purely coincidental.

The opinions expressed in this manuscript are solely the opinions of the author and do not represent the opinions or thoughts of the publisher. The author has represented and warranted full ownership and/or legal right to publish all the materials in this book.

This book may not be reproduced, transmitted, or stored in whole or in part by any means, including graphic, electronic, or mechanical without the express written consent of the publisher except in the case of brief quotations embodied in critical articles and reviews.

Outskirts Press, Inc.
http://www.outskirtspress.com

ISBN: 978-1-9772-1137-8

Library of Congress Control Number: 2019903984

Cover Image by 99designs

Outskirts Press and the "OP" logo are trademarks belonging to
Outskirts Press, Inc.

PRINTED IN THE UNITED STATES OF AMERICA

Contents

Editorial Preface by Lindsay Fitzgerald

Wanders Far—An Unlikely Hero's Journey was a treat for me to work on as editor because of its uniqueness. It is often the case in our lives that we read the same story over and over again, variations on a theme. Many stories seem to follow particular trajectories, as if written in paint-by-numbers. By contrast, *Wanders Far* is not just another variation on a story that you or I have read dozens of times before. It is a richly imagined world and cast of characters that arrives on the scene with a bounty of gifts for the reader to devour.

What is its genre—historical fiction, supernatural fiction, adventure, or mystery? It is all of them, and if you are a fan of any of these genres, *Wanders Far* will speak to you. The world of *Wanders Far* is both grounded in "reality" as we know it, and the supernatural. It is a mystical adventure that readers of adult fiction and young adult fiction alike can leap into.

This story and its characters transcend time. The book begins in the year 1,125, but the story is not constrained by its time period. The characters are written with such heart and emotional transparency that a contemporary reader can easily connect and resonate with them. The characters' journeys speak to the human experience throughout the ages. In the world of *Wanders Far*, we find elements of adventure, democracy, matriarchy, tragedy, triumph, family bonding, love, leadership, succession, community-building, and participatory decision-making. We also find elements of the otherworldly. I won't spoil the story for you by saying more on that score, but read on and prepare to feel the shiver up your spine.

And as for the ending? Do yourself a favor and resist the temptation to skip ahead. Page by page, the author leads us down a path that culminates in an ending you will not soon forget.

Preface and Dedication

This book is dedicated to the Wilmington Historical Society and their purpose, which is "to collect, preserve, display and interpret the documents, photographs and artifacts that tell the unique story of how the people of this remote, mountainous small town with big ideas have adapted and survived in the harsh but beautiful environment of the Adirondacks." It is also dedicated to their endeavor to build the Ruth and Thomas Keegan Memorial History Center along Route 86 in Wilmington, New York. Thanks to the hard work of president Karen Marshall Peters, the dedication of the officers and directors, the donations of members, and the generosity of its benefactor, Colonel Dennis Keegan, that dream is on the way to becoming reality.

The idea to write this book came to me while I was researching my first book, *In the Shadow of a Giant*, a book about my grandparents' business, set near Whiteface Mountain in the Adirondack Mountains of New York State during the 1960s and early 1970s. This book is set in New York State in the years from 1125 to 1192, some eight hundred years earlier.

Perhaps it is far-fetched to think that the legend of How Whiteface Mountain Got Its Name could be combined with the story of How the Haudenosaunee, pronounced Who-den-a-saw-knee, commonly known as Iroquois, Became the Confederacy of Five Tribes. Fortunately, that's just the sort of leap the author of an historical novel gets to make. It can't be proven, nor can it be disproven.

On the official website for the Whiteface Mountain Ski Center, there is a page which offers four theories for the original naming of the mountain. The fourth, and most intriguing theory, is attributed to an historical pamphlet published by High Falls Gorge, wherein the legend is entitled, "White Face Mountain, the Land of Romance." The webpage cites as sources the following members of the Wilmington Historical Society: Douglas Wolfe, Guy Stephenson, and Judy Lawrence. While I was thinking about telling that story my own way, I read the book *The Spirit of Whiteface: A Novella*, by Mike Bowman. I enjoyed his version of the Whiteface Mountain naming tale. This book goes in a very different direction. The main character in this book came to me during that time, and he compelled me to write his story, so perhaps he was not a fictional character.

After I wrote my first book, my brother Jeff told me that I should write a book like the ones I enjoyed growing up. As a kid, I read every book about Native American heroes I could find, heroes like Sitting Bull, Crazy Horse, Geronimo, Tecumseh, and Sacajawea. I also read westerns, from the Louis L'Amour catalog to James Michener's *Centennial*. With my brother's encouragement in mind, I came to think, "Maybe I could do that."

As for the history in this book, there are differences between accepted history and native legends. In particular, the stories passed down through the generations say that the unification of the tribes that make up the Iroquois nation culminated during an eclipse. Some believe that occurred in the 1400s (June 28, 1451). Others believe it occurred in the 1100s (August 22, 1142). Miraculously, scientists and mathematicians can recalculate the exact date and time of eclipses, hundreds and thousands of years ago. I wrote the first draft of this book thinking it was set in 1451, then I was more drawn to the idea and belief in the theory that the eclipse of 1142 was the date of the unification. Perhaps it doesn't make a difference to the reader. I subtracted the 309 years, although the later date theory is probably still more favored by historians.

The legend of the unification of tribes comes from the verbal tradition. Though there are many hypotheses about the actual people in the story, I have incorporated the more mainstream legends involving:

- Hiawatha, also known as He Who Seeks Wampum, which I shortened to Seeks Wampum
- The Peacemaker, also known as Two River Currents Flowing Together, or Two Rivers
- Todadaho, or Entangled, and
- She Who Lives Along the Road to War, or Road to War. In the course of the book she becomes New Face.

The main character of the book is a fictional young man, Wanders Far, and his fictional family, headed up by his mother, Bear Fat. I have set them within the Bear Clan village of the People of the Flint. I refer to them as the People of the Flint or simply the people instead of using the name Mohawk. Together I refer to the unified confederacy of tribes as the People of the Longhouse. The other tribes within the confederacy are referred to by the names Oneida, Onondaga, Cayuga, and Seneca. This book has been written using the English language as currently spoken, and it is understood that many words or concepts may not have existed within the people's language. The reader is asked to overlook that fact. Further, it was a challenge to refer to the many geographical settings in this book without using their modern names. In some cases, I renamed them, and in other cases I kept their modern names. I recognize that this could cause confusion. I refer to the Mohawk River as The People's River. I refer to the Hudson River as North River. I left the modern names for the following bodies of water: Garoga Creek, Moose River, Sacandaga River, Canandaigua Lake, Lake Champlain (or Champlain's Lake), Lake Ontario, Cazenovia Lake, and Copperas Pond which serves as the summer home base for the main characters of the book. I have also renamed some of New York state's most notable landmarks, for instance, The Great Roaring Waterfalls referred to in the book is Niagara Falls, and Cave Eye is Natural Stone Bridges and Caves in Pottersville, New York. The cliffs along Lake Ontario are located within Chimney Bluffs State Park.

I would like to add a deep expression of gratitude to my editor, Lindsay Fitzgerald. Lindsay has helped me realize my vision and has been an enthusiastic partner in every aspect of bringing this story to life. I would also like to thank and acknowledge the earliest readers and members of the launch team, including Patti Fitz-Gerald, Jane Peck, Maureen Miller, and Molly Mead.

The stunning design work by Juan Padrón captured the essence of the hero, and his cover design beckons the reader inside. Thank you, Juan.

Storytelling is a major theme in this book, and a couple of the major characters in the book had a gift for it. I love the audio book narration by Bill Buwalda; I could listen to him for hours. I think Hiawatha would be proud of the way Bill Buwalda made these words sing. Great job, Bill.

I have had a fantastic time dreaming up these characters and breathing life into them and their legends.

Chapter One
Grandfather Is Dead

A fly landed on her knee. She wondered how long she could tolerate its presence. How long could she keep her right leg from moving? It was such a tiny creature, yet the urge to flick it away consumed her thoughts. It took every ounce of fortitude she could muster. Why not shake it off and be done with it? There were far more important matters to tend to than playing a silly game with a tiny pest.

The fly had grown comfortable, and started rubbing his front legs together, like he was trying to keep his hands warm on a cold winter day, but it was only early autumn. It amazed her to think that such a tiny creature could tickle and distract her so completely.

From across the room her sister inquired, "Don't you agree, Bear Fat?"

Bear Fat's hand slapped her knee. Her hand moved with lightning speed, a skill perfected over the course of many years. The tiny red-eyed housefly landed dead on its back at Bear Fat's feet, instantly forgotten. The sudden smack of her hand on her bare knee was loud enough to jolt the gathering of women to attention. Their meeting had lasted for hours, and nobody had said anything new since the meeting began. Bear Fat couldn't recall when her sister had begun to speak.

At 34-years-old, she was a seasoned leader, great at listening to her people, and helping them participate in decisions that impacted them all. Ordinarily she had the capacity to sit for hours thinking through complex situations. She was patient when her people complained about little things or agonized over tough decisions. That particular afternoon her thoughts wandered.

Her people could easily overlook her distraction. Only weeks before, her youngest child had been snatched away. Bear Fat was busy collecting tubers, alone in the woods, and had left the baby safely in her papoose at the base of a tree a short distance from where she was digging. She saw it happen, but it happened so fast that she was powerless to stop the abduction. She ran in pursuit, and she screamed for her people's help but they were beyond the sound of her voice. She was the mother of six other children. Her sister told her she should take consolation in that. Bear Fat couldn't see how having six other children should diminish the loss of the baby she called Blackberry. The baby had a tiny birthmark on her left ankle that looked like a blackberry. Bear Fat told her sister, "It doesn't matter how many children she has, a baby needs its mother."

Bear Fat acknowledged that her sister was right to remind her of her responsibility to her people. Uniquely, the three clans of their people regarded their matriarch as their most important leader. She was even more important than the chief who was responsible for leading the men in defense of the village, and in their endeavors outside of the village. Her sister complimented her leadership, praising the fact that the people had never gone hungry during her many years as matriarch. As children they had known some very hungry years. The complimentary words of her sister sang in Bear Fat's ears, "Well fed, well led."

She couldn't do anything about her lost baby. She didn't even get a good enough look at the abductor to identify him or his people. She could grieve the loss of her baby and yet fully perform her job.

It was particularly helpful to be needed at that moment. Bear Fat sighed, and responded, "I don't know." She paused momentarily, then continued, "I just know we can't stay here any longer. It is time to move on. We have been happy here and moving is a chore, but resources are beginning to grow sparse. There are fewer fish in the river, fewer deer in our meadows, and we must travel ever farther to find wood for our fires and rabbits for our cookpots. We must find a new home. We will not go hungry again. Not while I have anything to say about it! Let's vote."

Bear Fat would have preferred to achieve unanimity. They would have to proceed without the consent of Bear Fat's sister. Her sister wasn't really opposed, she just had a difficult time committing to one alternative at the exclusion of another.

Just as Bear Fat closed the matter and prepared to adjourn the meeting, her 10-year-old son, Fisher, ran breathlessly through the doorway, skidding to a halt, and scaring up a cloud of light brown dust in front of his mother.

"Grandfather is dead," the boy shouted. "Come quick." He turned and ran back out through the doorway. Everyone followed. It was hard to keep up with him. Bear Fat shrieked and ran quickly behind Fisher.

About half a mile from the village, on the top of a small hill, a 50-year-old man lay crumpled on the ground. The old man's head was painted red, down to just beneath his nose. Beneath a line that extended from ear to ear, his face was painted pitch black. Near the line that separated the red and black, a row of tiny black dots had been painted over the red. Five evenly distributed, neatly braided lengths of freshly greased hair adorned his head. The braids sprouted from a spot on the top of his head near the back, and two small feathers from the wing of his namesake, the red-winged blackbird, had been carefully woven into the braids. That morning, his grandson had asked him to demonstrate how a warrior prepared for battle.

Fisher stood by his dead grandfather, pointing at the body, as if his mother and the others who had followed required such guidance. Everyone could plainly see that the man had died. Bear Fat dropped to the ground, cradled her father's head in the crook of her elbow, and with eyes full of tears she looked up and asked her son what happened.

Fisher said, "I don't know. We were just standing there on top of the hill, looking for rabbits, pheasants, or turkeys, anything worth notching an arrow for. Then he just dropped to the ground and was dead. So I started running and didn't stop until I got to the village." The boy tried hard not to cry. His mother's tears made it more difficult. He was getting to the age where he tried harder and harder to be like the men. Then he thought of his grandfather, and it occurred to Fisher that he would never see him again. He stood silently, tears streaming down his cheeks. He tucked his chin to his chest and stared at his toes.

Bear Fat asked Fisher, "Can you run and get your father? Tell him what has happened and tell him we need to bring Grandfather back to the village." The boy nodded and started running, happy to be on the move. Bear Fat and her sister straightened out their father's body to achieve a more dignified pose. Bear Fat closed her father's eyes, kissed his forehead, and then kissed each cheek. She touched the tip of her nose to the tip of his nose. Then she buried her face in her strong hands. She kneeled in the dirt by her father for a long time, until she became aware of her screaming mother running quickly up the hill. Bear Fat collected herself. Her mother, Gentle Breeze, and the rest of the village needed her to be strong. She cleared the tears from her eyes as best she could, her dusty hands leaving a coat of mud on her cheeks.

Bear Fat's husband, Big Canoe, arrived quickly with three other men and a wooden stretcher. Bear Fat and Big Canoe shared a quick embrace, and Big Canoe whispered condolences into her ear.

Bear Fat and her mother followed the men carrying Red-Winged Blackbird back to the village. Bear Fat held her sobbing mother's hand on the way back home. For her mother's sake, Bear Fat blinked back her own tears.

Red-Winged Blackbird had been a dutiful husband, father, and grandfather, and everyone in the village enjoyed his company. He was dependable, and he could be counted on in any situation. His unique talent was wood carving. As they passed through the wooden fences that surrounded and protected the village, Bear Fat blew a kiss at the sign that towered over the gate, as if the sign had suddenly come to possess the spirit of her father.

The village was a Bear Clan village, one of three prominent clans that made up their tribe. At the village entrance was a large round sign with a fierce depiction of a bear, standing upright, fangs bared, and claws ready to disembowel any unwelcome intruders. Each of the longhouses had a smaller sign of the totem animal, each in different settings.

Red-Winged Blackbird had been a gifted artisan. His work was everywhere in the village. In addition to the signs, he made more practical objects, such as wooden bowls, tools, and weapons. He was happiest making the decorative objects.

Ten days later, they buried Bear Fat's father beside the People's River. The grieving period was officially over. On the way back to the village, Bear Fat informed the chief that the Women's Council had decided to move the village. Twenty years in the same location was enough. The chief nodded, affirming that he had heard. Slowly he said, "We will begin making plans right away. Next spring, we will move. I will tell everyone in the morning."

Chapter Two
A Good Place to Start a New Life

The location they chose for the new village was almost ten miles up a tiny tributary of the People's River. It was a nice spot at the top of a hill. At the bottom of the hill, the tiny creek looped around, forming a large curve that almost doubled back on itself.

Winter came late, and it gave the men time to clear the trees and brush along the banks of the creek and the hillside above. It would take many trees to build a new village. Branches were trimmed from the fallen trees. Then the logs were cut to size. By spring they would be dry and ready to work with.

While the men worked on the trees, many children worked together to build a dam in the creek, a couple hundred yards north of the riverbend. It was the perfect spot for a dam. Behind the dam, they created a small pond, big enough to fit everyone, but just barely.

It was a long winter. People were hungry for something other than corn. There was much to do. A small group of hunters worked long days to feed the village, while everyone else labored at the new village site. The men and boys worked from dawn to dark building twelve new longhouses. The women and girls worked all day clearing the fields and preparing the soil by the creek for new garden plots. To assure the people would be fed the following winter, they also seeded the gardens in the old village, just in case the new garden plots failed to yield bumper crops.

Bear Fat's husband, Big Canoe, was an able builder. His strengths included crafting canoes, hunting bears, and constructing buildings. In addition to directing the husbands of Bear Fat's sisters, aunts, and cousins, Big Canoe had an army of boys to supervise as well.

Bear Fat and Big Canoe had six living children, three daughters and three sons. Their son Fisher was 11 that spring and worked with the men on building the walls and framing the roof. Their 9-year-old son worked on cutting long strips of bark from trees, which would be woven into the roof frame. Their 7-year-old son worked on collecting stones from the garden and dragging them up the hill to be used in the fireplace hearths in the new longhouses. Everyone had a role to play.

In the garden, Bear Fat and her daughters worked with the other women to prepare for planting. Bear Fat named her girls Corn, Bean, and Squash. It was her way of showing appreciation to the Great Spirit for the three crops that sustained the people. It was rare for names given at birth to continue into adulthood, but all three girls retained their original names. The girls were born one after the other. That spring, they were 19, 18, and 17-years-old. All three were married, and all were pregnant that spring. None were as far along as Bear Fat herself, who was pregnant again at 35-years-old.

Bear Fat's longhouse was the largest of the village's twelve longhouses. At 140 feet long, sixteen feet wide, and fifteen feet high, the new building would become home to fourteen families, seven on one side and seven on the other. Each family, regardless of size, occupied a length of twenty feet, and shared a fire in the middle with a related family on the other side.

After a couple weeks of building, Big Canoe was pleased with the progress. The building was going up quickly. The walls were nearly complete, and the roof was completely framed. He stood a short distance from the structure, hands on his hips. He enjoyed a brief rest and noticed the pleasant warm sunshine on his back as he thought about the work yet to be done. His crew was working hard and needed surprisingly little supervision.

Big Canoe watched as his second son bounded up a ladder to the top of the longhouse. He noticed the boy's agility. There was much work yet to do on the roof. Most of the men and boys moved slowly and carefully on the top of the building. Big Canoe chuckled as the thought came to him that his boy reminded him of a chipmunk. It struck him that he had never seen his son so happy as he looked scampering around on top of the longhouse.

When work paused at midday for a brief lunch break, Big Canoe talked to his son about the roof of the longhouse. The boy told his father that he wished he could sleep on the roof instead of in the longhouse.

"What are you, some kind of chipmunk?" his father joked. The boy smiled, pulled his hands up to his chest, extended his two front teeth over his lower lip, bent his waist, and stuck his butt out to represent a long, fluffy tail. From that moment on he was called Chipmunk. "I don't know about sleeping on the roof, but how about if we make you a place to sit up there? You can climb up and watch over the village and warn our people of any danger you might see approaching."

Instead of one chair, Big Canoe built four chairs and secured them on the roof. The four chairs were positioned so that Chipmunk could face whichever direction he pleased. It took the better part of two days for Big Canoe to add the perch to the longhouse. It was unlike any house the people had ever seen. Initially Chipmunk had to share the chairs with others, until the novelty wore off.

One after the other, as each longhouse was completed, the rest of the crew moved to assist with the remaining work. Bear Fat and Big Canoe's longhouse was the second-to-last house to be finished.

When the longhouses were finished, work began on building the palace walls, just like at the old village, they built an outer ring first, then they built an inner ring five feet away. Bear Fat stood proudly as the sign from the old village was mounted above the gate to the new village. The men looked to Bear Fat when the installation was complete. Bear Fat nodded her approval, then she blew a kiss at the sign, a practice that was quickly becoming a habit. Every time she did that, she thought of her father.

It was about a month before the spring solstice. The new village was finished. All that was left to do was move everything that remained in the old village.

It was a lot of work. The trail between the old village and the new village became very well worn. A few of the older people had remained behind while the new village was being built. Bear Fat's mother was one of them. Gentle Breeze was a happy, healthy, 51-year-old great-grandmother. She still mourned the loss of her husband who had died the previous fall and being alone in the longhouse at the old village had left her feeling lonely. She had been accustomed to tending the hearth and preparing meals for Bear Fat and her large family. Gentle Breeze dedicated her time to keeping the old village spotlessly clean while her people spent two months building the new village. Bear Fat knew better than to ask her mother why she would devote so much time to keeping a place clean that no one would occupy again.

Bear Fat's eyes met her mother's. She smiled warmly, and softly said, "Mother, it is time to go." The final parade from the old village began. Their chief ceremonially led the way. Gentle Breeze and Bear Fat brought up the rear. Bear Fat's position as matriarch was even more important to the people than the chief's role, and it was fitting that the entire tribe marched between their chief and their matriarch.

Bear Fat kept up with her people. She had made the ten mile

walk many times over the previous couple of months as they prepared to move. That final walk was a lot more challenging. She
hadn't mentioned it to anyone. About half way to the new village,
it became clear to Bear Fat that her baby was on the way. For weeks
she had wondered, would the baby be born in the old village or the
new village? She hadn't thought to wonder whether the baby would
be born on the path between villages, but that was exactly what happened. She believed everything in life had meaning. Bear Fat wondered what it meant that her baby would be born along the trail.
One day she would come to know.

Seven miles down the path, Bear Fat told her mother the baby
was coming. Another mile down the path, she stopped in a small
clearing in the woods where the ferns gave way to moss and grass.
She thought it looked like a good place to start a new life. With her
mother's help, Bear Fat gave birth to another son. There was no such
thing as an effortless labor, but that boy came fast. So that's what
she called him: Fast. Bear Fat liked one-word names for her babies.
Her new boy was a strong, healthy, good-looking baby. Bear Fat and
Gentle Breeze shared a warm glance. Bear Fat sent her thoughts to
the Great Spirit: "May he serve our people well."

Then they were only three hours behind the rest of the village.
Bear Fat wrapped her baby in a tiny blanket and placed him between
her breasts, his small head tilted sideways against her chest, and
the tiny black smudge of hair on his head tickled her chin. Gentle
Breeze helped lift Bear Fat's pack on to Bear Fat's back, then picked
up her own heavily laden basket. Bear Fat couldn't wait to get to the
new village and introduce her new baby to their people. Having just
given birth, it took Bear Fat and Gentle Breeze a long time to walk
the final two miles.

Chapter Three
Runaway Toddler

I t was a brutally hot, late summer day, the following year. Bear Fat was working in a large garden, harvesting corn from her family's enormous plot along the banks of Garoga Creek. Two newborn infants squirmed side by side on a deerskin hide in the middle of their family's field, under the watchful eyes of the hard-working women. Bear Fat's 1-year-old toddler had been playing quietly near the infants.

Until he went missing.

Squash sounded the alarm. Bear Fat screamed and set out in search of her missing son, who had attempted to escape the sweltering field dozens of times that day. She searched nearby, then she searched farther afield. She circled the garden plot, and then she quickly followed the trail up the hill that overlooked the creek. From the top of the hill she saw him, standing on a rock at the edge of the pond behind the dam above the garden plots. She let out another loud scream, and set off at a dead run back down the hill, through the fields of corn, then along the bank of the creek to a distance way beyond that which a tiny toddler should be able to waddle before being noticed as missing.

When Bear Fat reached the pond, her son was seated on the rock, preparing to slide from the rock into the deep water on the other side. She admonished herself with a disgusted sigh for having lost sight of the boy, but at the same time she knew she was lucky to have reached him just when she did. She picked him up, sat on the rock, and let him nurse. It had been hours since she had taken a break, and it felt nice to sit on the rock with her feet in the water. When her son was finished nursing, she felt a need to cool off. She waded into the water, and the baby giggled when the cool water submerged him to his chin. Bear Fat made cooing noises and giggled at her last little boy. That afternoon she decided she would call him Wanders Far, replacing the name she gave him the day he was born.

It wasn't long before the other women found their way down the path, one after the next, as they noticed that Bear Fat hadn't returned. The last woman brought the infants and placed them on their deerskin at the side of the river before she joined her mother, sisters, aunts, and cousins. The idea of a swim was infectious that afternoon, and soon every woman and child from the village was up to her ears in the cool water.

Gentle Breeze had been tending to the tidiness of Bear Fat's longhouse most of the day, sticking to a routine of cleaning things every day whether they needed it or not. Eventually, the noise at the river drew Gentle Breeze outside and down the trail to the creek. She was the last woman to arrive. After a brief swim, Gentle Breeze sat on the large rock, with her feet in the water, hands on her cheeks, palms joined at her chin, forearms covering her bare breasts, and tears in her eyes, overcome with pride and gratitude watching her hardworking family and friends enjoy themselves in the water.

When the men and older boys returned from their work in the woods, they heard the fun at the river from a great distance. It wasn't long before they were enjoying the cool water as well. Though it was late in the season, it was the hottest day of the year.

All day, women carried baskets full of corn up the hill. By the end of the day, the storage spaces in the longhouses were full. There was corn hanging from every post and pole. It was piled high in every nook and cranny, even in the sleeping bunks, leaving just barely enough room for the people to sleep between stacks of corn. Hordes of corn were buried in subterranean caches. As a precaution, in case the village should burn, some of the caches were located outside the village. It was such a bountiful harvest, it seemed like corn was everywhere.

After their swim, on the way through the fields, the women picked up their remaining baskets and carried them up the hill.

Chapter Four
Too Many Trout to Count

As soon as the snow melted the following spring, and the ice on the ponds was gone, Bear Fat couldn't wait to get out of the village. Every year, Bear Fat and her immediate family left the village and traveled to a small wickiup, or wigwam, on a beautiful large pond at the foot of a majestic mountain, 120 miles to the north of their village on Garoga Creek. Bear Fat hadn't missed a year since she married Big Canoe when she was 16-years-old, and Big Canoe hadn't missed a year since he was born. Bear Fat enjoyed taking a couple of months away from her duties as matriarch, and she enjoyed getting out of the confines of the village as well. Living in a house with fifty other people made Bear Fat yearn for the great outdoors and summer in the mountains. She didn't mind the long walk, hard work, and miles of paddling or carrying a canoe to get to their destination. Most years they were able to make the trip a leisurely expedition.

That year, Bear Fat and Big Canoe traveled with Squash and her young family. Her husband Flint was from the Turtle Clan village, ten miles to the southwest of Garoga Creek. Squash and Flint had a 2-year-old son, named Pine Cone. He was born a couple of months after Wanders Far. The journey north also included Bear Fat and Big Canoe's boys, Fisher, Chipmunk, Dandelion, and Wanders Far, aged 13, 11, 9, and 2.

Everything was packed. They said their goodbyes, strapped their mostly empty, big woven baskets onto their backs, and headed north. If all went well, the baskets would be packed with valuable provisions when they returned.

Almost a week later, they arrived at Copperas Pond. It had been a few years since Squash made the trip, deciding to remain at Garoga Creek after she got married. When their wickiup finally came into view, she stopped momentarily, and tears filled her eyes at the sight of the small, familiar structure in the clearing by the pond. She hadn't realized how much she had missed it. She set her pack down by the fire pit and sat on a log bench. Her husband sat next to her. She looked out across the water. Then she glanced at him to see if she could tell what he was thinking since Flint had never been to Copperas Pond before.

The next day, everyone got to work collecting materials to make a canoe. Big Canoe, Flint, and Fisher located a tall, straight, mature birch tree. Big Canoe instructed Flint to notch it on one side, and then to chop with his axe on the other side. Next, they cut a long straight incision in the bark, with a bent-handled knife. They took the whole length of bark, from the bottom of the trunk almost all the way to the top of the tree. Using their fingers, they gently peeled the bark from the tree, working slowly and carefully to prevent ripping the bark. On occasions when the bark got stuck, they dislodged it by using a thin piece of bark as a scraper. When the bark was entirely separated from the tree, they rolled the bark and used twine to tie the rolled bark for transport back to camp. Then they chopped down several cedar trees.

Meanwhile, the others dug up long lengths of white spruce roots. The spruce roots would become stitching and would be used for lashing.

When they had enough spruce root, they gathered globs of hardened spruce resin to make glue. Bear Fat used a long stick to knock hardened globs of resin from high points in the trees, and the young boys scrambled to retrieve them when they hit the ground. Squash used a knife to cut globs that were within her natural reach. When they finished collecting the resin, Squash used her knife to cut everyone a small piece of spruce resin chewing gum.

Back at their camp on Copperas Pond, Big Canoe had a special workspace for building canoes. In addition to having everything he needed close at hand, rocks and roots had been removed from the soil so the ground could be used to hammer in the stakes that would serve as supports for the shaping of the canoe as it was built.

With the materials gathered, Big Canoe, Flint, and the older boys set out in search of bears. Bear Fat and Squash worked on processing the canoe materials.

Dandelion's job was to feed the family. For a couple of weeks that spring, Dandelion spent most of the day fishing. Every day, Squash would ask her baby brother, Wanders Far, "How many fish do you think Dandelion will bring us today?" Sometimes Squash would count with him until he said stop. Other times, he would use his fingers to make his prediction. The first day, he correctly guessed fourteen. Squash thought it was amusing that he made such a lucky guess. The second day he guessed twenty-two. She thought that it was quite a coincidence. The third day he guessed five. Squash was stunned. "How do you know, Wanders Far?"

The little boy said, "I don't know. I just know everything he thinks."

"Really," Squash inquired, "what is Dandelion thinking right now?"

Wanders Far said, "His foot hurts. He hit a rock."

Squash looked at Dandelion. "Well, what were you thinking?"

Dandelion shrugged and said, "It's true. I stubbed my toe. I was clumsy, and I wasn't looking where I was going. I was thinking that I wished my toe didn't hurt so much."

Squash looked back at Wanders Far and asked, "Do you know what other people think?"

Wanders Far shook his head back and forth, "No. Just Dandelion." Though seven years separated them, they shared a close bond.

Squash decided to stop asking how many fish Dandelion caught. She was getting tired of trout anyway. Pine Cone had scampered off down a trail, and Squash set off to retrieve him. When she returned, Wanders Far was sitting silently on the ground with a distant look in his eyes. She watched him for a few minutes. His eyes fluttered, but he didn't move a muscle. Squash said his name. She raised her voice to attract his attention. He was unresponsive. She became concerned. She touched his shoulder to get his attention. When she touched him, she felt a tiny spark on her skin. She jumped back, startled by the sensation. Wanders Far turned to look at her.

Squash blurted, "What just happened?"

Wanders Far said, plainly, "I just got back. That little bird took me on a trip in the sky." He pointed to a small gray and white Dark-eyed Junko perched on the branch of a shrub on the edge of the camp clearing.

"Oh he did, did he! Maybe next time I'll go too." Squash chided him and then returned to her work.

While Dandelion was fishing, Bear Fat and Squash got as much work done as they could while tending to the active toddlers. They seeped the spruce roots in hot water until they became pliable. Then the bark was stripped from the roots. The spruce resin was heated in a porous bag in a pot. They used a stick to push the bag to the bottom of the pot, and used a ladle to skim the clear, pure, gum from the surface of the pot. Then the gum was poured into clean cold water where it hardened immediately. Then the gum was pulled and extruded by hand, over and over until it was a perfect color and consistency. Later when they needed to waterproof the seams and caulk the canoe, the pulled gum would be further processed by adding tallow, or animal fat in just the right amount to prevent degrading the adhesive qualities at high and low temperatures. Bear Far had to admit that converting the resin to an adhesive was not her favorite task, but she was proud of the family's tradition of building at least one canoe per year. She was also proud of Big Canoe's reputation for building the highest quality boats.

It took several weeks, but eventually the men took four medium-sized bears. While Bear Fat and Squash worked on processing the bears, Big Canoe turned to woodworking. First, he crafted the keel, which would run along the bottom of the canoe, from bow to stern. Then he crafted the gunnel from two long cedar strips that he slowly bent by hand in warm water. The gunnel would eventually become the eye-shaped frame along the perimeter on the top of the canoe. Next, he worked on fashioning strips of cedar into what would become the ribs of the canoe. At every step in the process, Big Canoe closely inspected each building component, and clearly enjoyed doing the work of a craftsman. A series of satisfied, affirmative grunts always signaled satisfaction.

When everything was ready, Big Canoe began assembling all the parts into a finished canoe. With the help of his family, it came together efficiently. Bear Fat and Squash used bone awls to poke holes into the birch bark and used the spruce roots as stitching to sew the seams. Big Canoe and his helpers were constantly using stakes hammered into the ground to carefully bend, shape, and bind the wooden materials into the perfect position to achieve the shape that they needed. Big Canoe cut the bark at the bow in the shape of a crescent so the canoe would glide effortlessly across the surface of the water. Then Bear Fat finished stitching the bark at the bow.

As the canoe neared completion, Bear Fat heated the glue and added the tallow, and then she covered every stitch and seam with the protective adhesive. Big Canoe used a soft wooden mallet to knock the ribs into place and lash the last remaining structural components perfectly into place.

When the canoe was finished and the glue had dried, it was time for the final test. Big Canoe always enjoyed taking the latest canoe for a ride, slowly and proudly showing the family the finished results of their collective handiwork. Everyone was happy on boat launch day, especially Bear Fat. She stood with hands on her hips, watching as her husband darted back and forth along the shore of the small pond. Every year the test passed. Never once had a finished canoe required additional work. That afternoon Big Canoe made his second pass along the shore, grinning proudly. It happened quickly, and in the course of seconds his expression darkened. The canoe's forward progress halted, then it sank. Bear Fat dropped to a crouch, cupped her cheeks in her hands, astonished. She was sure that it was her work that was defective. She had been looking forward to moving on to more agreeable work. Instead she spent most of the next two days carefully repairing the rip and waterproofing the stitches again.

Most years, the summer hunt was processed, and the canoe was finished about six weeks before the autumn equinox. The final summer task was collecting and drying blueberries, which the family enjoyed doing at a comfortable pace. While the rest of the family worked on blueberry picking, Big Canoe and Flint stayed behind at camp, guarding their valuable meat supply. Big Canoe thought of those last summer days before returning home to Garoga Creek as his time to be lazy for a couple of days. Big Canoe and Flint spent most of those days sitting in the pond instructing the toddlers. By the time summer ended, Wanders Far and Pine Cone were proficient swimmers.

Chapter Five
Ambushed

The following year, late in the afternoon on an unseasonably warm autumn day, 12-year-old Chipmunk was enjoying some quiet time to himself on the roof of the longhouse. He had long since developed the custom of sitting first in one chair on the roof, then switching to the next until he had spent a substantial amount of time in each of the four chairs his father had installed on the roof three years earlier. At peace with his thoughts, undisturbed by the noise of the village below, Chipmunk carefully surveyed the distant horizons. Sometimes Chipmunk would prepare the village for the arrival of foul weather. Occasionally he was able to direct hunters to deer in the distance. That afternoon, he saw a faint blur to the west.

Chipmunk strained and squinted. It was smoke! Smoke, where smoke shouldn't be. He jumped from his chair and scampered down the ladder steps on the side of the longhouse. Moments later, he was back on the roof with his father.

"Nice job, Son!" Big Canoe smiled at the boy and he was off to inform the chief. Chipmunk remained on the roof and watched as a dozen men from the village set out to determine whether the village was in danger. While the scouts were away, the rest of the village prepared for the worst. It didn't take long, since the village was almost always prepared for the worst.

An hour and a half later, a pair of scouts returned to update the chief. They spied about a dozen Hurons around a fire, tending their weapons, with three fresh scalps and a severed head in their possession. They were too busy bragging and telling stories to know they had been spied by the people's scouts.

The next morning, the raiding war party was ambushed halfway to the village by three dozen men, all growling like bears, and shooting arrows at the advancing party. One of the Hurons was killed. The rest of the war party managed to flee.

Back at Garoga Creek, the dead Huron was tied to a pole, for all to see. Big Canoe took Chipmunk to see the dead body of the enemy who would have attacked their village. Big Canoe praised his son and told him that due to his diligence, one Huron was dead and everybody in their village was safe. Furthermore, those enemies would think twice before coming back to attack the Bear Clan. Certainly, there were easier targets than the village at Garoga Creek.

Chipmunk smiled. He felt grateful to know that his favorite activity, sitting lazily on the roof watching over the safety of the village, was actually useful and appreciated by his friends and family.

Chapter Six
Swamp Creature

Regardless of the weather, every morning Bear Fat walked through the entire village. She entered each longhouse through the door on one end, had a cheerful greeting for everyone she came in contact with, and exited each longhouse from another door on the opposite end from which she had entered. If, for some strange reason, she missed making her tour in the morning, she would pass through in the afternoon or early evening. Often, Wanders Far would go with his mother when she made her daily walk.

It was a warm, early spring day, and Bear Fat's visits took longer than usual. She wanted to make sure everyone knew that she would be away for a couple of days. Bear Fat and her family were planning a trip to a small pond about thirty miles to the north of the village to gather clay. Several other women and their families were making the trip as well. The village's potters were out of clay.

Bean, Bear Fat's second daughter, was a gifted craftsperson. She understood that the village's families needed pottery for their utilitarian needs. She knew she could work faster if everything she made was plain and simple. Even so, Bean was compelled to decorate each pot, bowl, covered dish, mug, and pitcher. She was constantly looking for unique ways to combine materials and create one-of-a-kind objects that would be useful and beautiful. It didn't matter to her that she could have been twice as proficient. It didn't occur to Bean that the other women in her family had to work harder because Bean spent so much extra time at her craft.

Most of the time the potters worked together under a big tree just outside the palisade walls. The potters' guild included two older women and two younger women. An old woman, named Crane on account of her long neck, and a middle-aged woman called Woman of Few Words, were the veteran potters. Bean and her cousin Robin's Egg completed the pottery crew.

As she made her rounds, Bear Fat heard many requests for clay objects. She also checked on Crane and Woman of Few Words to make sure they would be ready to depart on time. Crane was a bossy and particular sort of woman, and she made sure that Bear Fat told her every detail of the trip plan. Woman of Few Words was packed for the trip and her family was ready to go, hours early. Bear Fat toured her own longhouse last. Robin's Egg's compartment looked orderly and she seemed to be finalizing her family's preparations.

In Bean's compartment, the preparation process was frantic. As usual, she waited too long to get started, and instead of quietly gathering things together, Bean talked non-stop, without regard for whether anyone was even listening. Bear Fat asked her daughter if there was anything she could do to help. Instead of telling her mother what she needed, Bean told Bear Fat what she had done. Bear Fat smiled warmly and told her daughter to let her know if she could help, and then completed her rounds.

The potters and their families hiked twenty miles that afternoon, stopping in a woodland glade by a small stream. They made a comfortable campsite for the evening. There was a small fire and someone was making a thick stew for dinner. They gathered around the fire, and the sun was beginning to set. Bear Fat stood by the stream by herself, not too far away. She reflected on the trip from

Garoga Creek, her hands on her hips, her knees bent slightly, shaking her head from side to side at the thought of her daughter Bean. Bean talked the entire trip. She had always been that way, Bear Fat supposed, but somehow she had forgotten just how talkative Bean was, now that Bean had her own family and her own compartment at the other end of their longhouse. Or maybe Bean had become even more talkative than when she was growing up. Bear Fat smiled slightly at the thought that although Bean had talked non-stop for twenty miles, Bear Fat couldn't recall one thing that her daughter had said. "What kind of leader am I?" thought Bear Fat, who considered that her most important duty as matriarch was to be a good listener. "What kind of mother am I?" she muttered to herself. Bear Fat shrugged at the thought, and it occurred to her that as long as her daughter and her daughter's family were happy, and as long as they had the luxury of being able to follow their passions, what more could she wish for as a mother? It always made Bear Fat happy when Bean showed off her latest, unique creations, and it made Bear Fat proud to think of the daily use those items would serve.

Bear Fat finished her contemplative moment, and then helped Big Canoe gather thick mats of moss from large stones in the woods by the creek. The moss was collected so they could wrap the clay to keep it moist for the trip home.

The next day they finished their trek to the familiar little pond. After they arrived, and the families got settled in for the day, Bear Fat walked a short distance from the pond, up a small hill. The hill and the pond were clear of trees, and Bear Fat loved to stand on the hill, looking down at the sweet little pond. It was shaped exactly like a duck. She didn't stay long. There was much work to do. Their empty baskets would be filled with all the dense, heavy, wet clay they could carry.

Bear Fat watched as her son Wanders Far found a large turtle near the pond. Turtle soup would make a nice addition to their evening picnic, she thought, as she raced down the hill to help steer the creature into the cook pot.

They worked diligently for several hours, then spent a couple of hours swimming before dinner. Nobody was in a hurry to get out of the water on that warm spring afternoon. Mostly they stood around in the pond, water up to their shoulders, their feet in the clay at the bottom of the pond, making scrunchy faces at the thought of the squishy clay oozing between their toes at the bottom of the water. Bear Fat looked at the water—milky, gray, the color of slate.

Wanders Far asked his mother, "Does the clay grow back each year after we take it, or does it push back up from underground?" Bear Fat couldn't answer that question, and nobody else had a helpful answer either. Fortunately, the small pond seemed to have an abundance of clay, and there was no need to worry about running out. Wanders Far sat at the edge of the pond and completely covered his body with a thick layer of clay. Bean admonished, "When that hardens, you'll be trapped in there, and we won't be able to get you out!"

Wanders Far was curious to see if his sister was right. She was an expert with clay, he thought. She should know. He hesitated momentarily. Then he committed himself to his experiment anyhow.

"You look like a gray ghost, or a swamp creature," Bean told Wanders Far at dinner. Everyone laughed at the observation. There was no denying what she said.

After dinner Wanders Far told Bear Fat about a dream he had. In the dream he was caked in mud, swimming in darkness. He was being chased by evil birds that wanted to rip him apart with their talons. He sounded scared.

Bear Fat reassured him, "We all have scary dreams sometimes. Usually we don't remember them when we wake up, but sometimes we do."

"But I wasn't sleeping when I had the dream," Wanders Far said.

Bear Fat reassured her son by telling him he had a very active imagination.

As the travelers settled down for another night of sleeping out in the open air, Bear Fat and Big Canoe sat beside the pond. They watched as a pair of Mallard ducks made their last swim of the day, followed by eight fuzzy chicks. "They have eight children too," Big Canoe pointed out.

Bear Fat smiled. She thought of their abducted baby, as she often did. She said a silent, hopeful prayer for her safety and well-being. Then she said, "We should thank the Great Spirit for putting a family of ducks on a pond shaped like a duck! And we should thank the Great Spirit for the ducks' beautiful chicks, as well as our own wonderful children." Then they watched the sun set over the horizon.

Early the next morning, the travelers set out for home. The heavy clay in their packs would make it a grueling trip, but the village would have plenty of material to keep the potters busy. Bear Fat closed her eyes for a moment and pictured them under their shade tree, just outside the palisade walls, hunched over their work, fingers, hands, and arms covered with the goopy gray clay. Then she opened her eyes and saw Wanders Far, coated in dried clay, a little cracked at the elbows, wrists, knees, and toes. Bear Fat's eyes met Wanders Far's eyes, and they grinned at each other.

Bean scowled at her brother and curled her lip. Then she said, "Just look at you! You're still covered with that clay." She hoisted her heavy pack to her back, grunted, and continued admonishing her brother for several minutes before another topic caught her fancy.

Bear Fat and Wanders Far walked faster than Bean, and it didn't take long before they were separated by enough distance that Bean couldn't hear them. Bear Fat whispered to her son, "I don't care what Bean says. You look great. I wish I had covered myself in clay too."

Chapter Seven
The Fierce Scream of a Fisher Cat

W anders Far proved more and more worthy of his name as he grew older. Bear Fat was constantly losing track of him and attempts to assign his brothers to attend to his whereabouts proved unsuccessful. Sometimes the entire village was called to search for him.

One day while everyone was gathering for dinner, it became clear that nobody had seen Wanders Far since the first thing that morning. Wanders Far was merely 5-years-old. Everyone thought somebody else was assigned to watch out for him that day. His brother, Dandelion, who was seven years older, shared the opinion that his brother ought to know better than to wander off by himself anyhow. Instead of enjoying a well-deserved meal, the family spent hours searching the village for the stray boy. Then they searched the fields and the creek. Their search expanded to a greater and greater radius, as the family searched for the trail of the missing boy. Fortunately, it was late spring. The days had grown longer, and sunset was later than usual, but as the sun dropped over the horizon, Wanders Far still had not been found.

The search continued even after the sun set. It was a clear night, but the going was slowed by the lack of light. The wide sky was full of brilliantly twinkling stars, yet all together they provided a fairly meager measure of illumination.

A terrifying, ear piercing scream rang out through the forests and fields. It sounded like one of the searchers was in the process of meeting a dreadfully gruesome end. All at once, Bear Fat darted off down a well-worn path toward the Wolf Clan village.

The fierce scream was the unmistakable sound of a fisher cat. It was unmistakable, except Bear Fat knew the difference. A couple of minutes later, Bear Fat found her oldest son and her youngest son walking hand in hand down the dirt path that connected their villages. Bear Fat was so happy to see her boys, she forgot all about how distraught she had been, and she forgot that the rest of the village was searching for her son as well. After a joyful reunion and some smothering motherly hugs, Fisher suggested getting Wanders Far home. The young boy was naked, tired, and dusty, though he denied being tired, even as he yawned mightily. They started back along the path toward the Bear Clan village, and as they went along, crowds of searchers fell in with them. The celebrations of the noisy crowd quieted as they dissipated once they reached the village. Gentle Breeze met them just outside their longhouse, overjoyed to see both of her grandsons, and ready for a hungry family. She had kept dinner fresh and warm, just the right distance from the fire.

After the family ate, Big Canoe asked Wanders Far to tell his glorious story of exploration. The boy explained that he had mostly just goofed off all day. First he made an entire village of tiny longhouses out of sticks and twigs in the dirt by the creek until he got bored with building. Then he took a short nap and had a bad dream about an evil chief with long messy hair full of burdocks. Wanders Far explained that the chief punched him, and he pointed to a scrape on his thigh where he hit the ground after being punched. Then he got the idea of going to visit his brother, Fisher.

After some laughter, all around the fire, Fisher took over. "You can't get a real-life injury by getting punched in a dream, Wanders Far." The others nodded in agreement.

Fisher went on and told his family how Wanders Far wandered into the Wolf Clan village in the middle of the afternoon, then wandered from house to house. Nobody paid too much attention to him until finally someone did, and thought to wonder whose child didn't know enough to know where he was. Wanders Far explained who he was, where he was from, and who he was looking for. Fisher put one of his hands on each of his little brother's shoulders, gave him a single, gentle shake, and proclaimed that Wanders Far was destined to be a runner, a traveler, a messenger between villages, and perhaps between tribes! Wanders Far nodded vigorously and smiled. It had never occurred to him before, but when his brother said it, he knew. That was exactly what he wanted to do, and he couldn't wait to get started.

Then Fisher went on to tell his family about their friends, and extended family who lived in the Wolf Clan village, a couple of miles to the northeast. The update went on for some time, and it wasn't long before Wanders Far fell fast asleep at his mother's side, near the fire. He saved the best part of his update for last. Fisher was going to be a father.

Big Canoe scooped up his little sleeping son and lifted him up to his bunk in their compartment of the longhouse. Then he followed Bear Fat, Gentle Breeze, and his three older sons down the length of the longhouse, sharing the news with the families of Bear Fat's daughters, sisters, aunts, and cousins.

It was well after midnight when Fisher climbed up to his boyhood bunk. It felt strange to sleep there. As he fell asleep, he thought about becoming a father. Only six months earlier, he had been a kid himself. He smiled and drifted off to sleep. A couple hours later, his feet were on the path, awake before everyone else in a village where everyone woke up early. It was great to visit his birth village, but he couldn't wait to get back home.

In the Wolf Clan village, he was a man.

Chapter Eight
Trading with the Narraganset

One day, near the start of autumn, a strange man from a distant land approached their village, hollering a friendly greeting as a proper visitor should. He introduced himself as Quahog. He carried a heavy pack and asked if anyone in the village wanted to trade.

Quahog was escorted to the center of the village, and the people began to assemble. Women brought cook pots from their lodge fires, and set them up at the communal fire pit. It was quickly becoming clear it would be an afternoon of leisure.

Quahog told everyone about his home near the ocean, where salt water crashed on a sandy beach. He told his hosts about how his people busied themselves gathering clams in the rivers and streams that emptied into the ocean. He described the tedious work of carving the small portion of the shells that was purple from the rest of the clamshell, and then the painstaking task of drilling a tiny hole through the cylindrically carved and polished shells. Quahog told everyone about his people, the Narraganset. He shared his own life story, and the life story of every member of his family, as well as most of the residents of his village.

The valuable shells were rapidly becoming currency for all tribes. In addition to their beauty and utility in wampum belts, they were small, rare, and tradable. The people listened intently as Quahog explained the work his people did to gather them and fashion them into beads.

Bear Fat and her family had recently returned from their annual summer trip to Copperas Pond. It was a very productive summer. They had triple the normal supply of dried blueberries, and double the normal supply of bear meat, bearskins, bear fat, and rendered oil. She traded a large bearskin, and the skin of a bear cub for an enormous sack of wampum beads, which she gave to her daughter Squash, the weaver in her family. Several other families made trades as well, and Quahog had a large basket of treasure to return home with.

Then Quahog inquired about other villages in the region. He still had a substantial quantity of beads. Wanders Far offered to take Quahog to his brother Fisher's village. Quahog put a few beads in Wanders Far's hand and winked at the boy. Wanders Far said in amazement, "I would have brought you there for nothing," and then he thanked the man. Then he added, "If you still have any more shells after that, there's another village near us, a bit farther, in the opposite direction." Everyone laughed, amused at Wander's Far's optimism and eagerness to help.

By the time Quahog had visited the three villages, he had purchased two large basket backpacks and filled them with the skins of animals, some of which he had never seen or heard of before, and a bounty of other provisions, including a special gift for his mother. In the middle of one of the backpacks full of skins was a large, carefully wrapped pitcher, with small river stones pressed into the bottom, and a pattern of ferns etched into the sides. It was one of Bean's most intricate creations.

With the last of his beads, Quahog hired Chipmunk and Dandelion to travel with him and carry the packs all the way to his home. Wanders Far begged and pleaded to join them. He was eager to see the enormous ocean and the waves which Quahog had described. Bear Fat convinced Wanders Far he would have to see it another year. She had important work for him to do while his brothers were away.

Chapter Nine
Choosing a New Chief

The following fall, Wanders Far was 7-years-old. He was a little old to sit at his mother's side during Women's Council meetings. She had convinced him that he could do important work for her, relaying messages whenever it was necessary.

Their chief had died the day before. The people's mourning process had begun. The Women's Council was meeting to consider alternatives. They were forbidden to make a decision until the ten-day grieving rituals were finished.

Bear Fat's partner in governance had come down with the flu. After a couple of days, he seemed to get sicker, rather than getting better. After that he declined quickly, and nobody seemed to be able to find a way to help him get better. Bear Fat sent for the medicine men from their neighboring villages to assist the Bear Clan's healer. Between the three of them, nothing seemed to work, or even help. It was no use.

The chief was not old enough for the women to have given considerable attention to the need for a succession plan. They began their council meeting by letting each woman speak as long as she wished. Some talked about their sadness at the loss of their chief. Some talked about the qualities a new chief should possess. Some talked about the qualities a new chief should definitely *not* possess.

There were twenty women in the council, so it took all morning to complete the process.

In the afternoon, the women methodically discussed every man in the village, excluding none, from the very young to the very old. At the mention of each man, the women voted. Unanimity was required. If even one woman voted no, that man was excluded from being a candidate. Before the voting began, Bear Fat warned that if they were too picky, they might not have any candidates. If they were uncertain, it was better to vote yes, to have them be a candidate, and then eliminate them later in the process. At the end of the day, they had eight candidates. The women took a vow of secrecy and returned to their longhouses for the evening.

At the end of the mourning period, the people buried their chief. Immediately the women went back to work. One of the main functions of the chief was to protect the people, so it was inherently unsafe to continue long without a chief.

One by one, the women sent Wanders Far to bring the men they had selected as candidates. Most were surprised to learn they were being considered. Some who expected to be considered were surprised to find they were not considered.

The interviews took many hours. Each man stood in front of the Women's Council and answered every question the women could think to ask. At the end of the day, the women voted again. As before, unanimity was required. Any woman could vote no, and the contestant would be eliminated, for any reason, or no reason at all. No explanation was ever required. The field was reduced to three.

Old Club was a well-respected warrior who had been a part of every battle, raid, skirmish, and defensive action for thirty-five years. He remained strong and athletic in spite of his 60 years. He was a white-haired veteran fighter. Old Club was a true survivor, and younger warriors were smart to listen to his advice and learn from Old Club's past experience.

The next oldest warrior in the tribe was twelve years younger than Old Club. He Who Makes Big Plans was a brilliant tactician who could quickly consider many alternatives and differentiate between the relative pros and cons to maximize chances for success. He enjoyed preparing war parties with detailed battle plans, drawing them in the dirt with a stick. Big Plans and Old Club always worked well together, and together they were the departed chief's top leaders.

Black Walnut was only 26-years-old. He knew at a young age he wanted to be a warrior. At 15, Black Walnut married Bear Fat's oldest daughter, Corn, and moved from the neighboring Turtle Clan village to Garoga Creek. Black Walnut was a fast learner, and proficient in all aspects of warrior service. He quickly gained the confidence of the chief. He was also well-respected by Big Plans and Old Club. Black Walnut's most useful talent was teaching, training, coaching, and mentoring the younger warriors. It was a hard profession to teach. Some of the young warriors proved challenging, overly eager to make a name for themselves, aggressive, and reckless. Black Walnut was patient, friendly, kind, and relatable, yet when a young warrior needed to be reined in, Black Walnut was able to command their compliance and respect. Although ten years did not seem a long time, already more than half of the warriors in the village had received their training from Black Walnut.

That morning, Corn was cleaning up after serving her family breakfast. Her three young sons were just getting ready to go outside, and her baby daughter was propped up against the bunks in her papoose facing the fire. Black Walnut was sitting in front of the fire crafting a bow from an ash sapling. When Wanders Far entered their compartment and said, "Black Walnut, the Women's Council would like to talk to you at once," Corn and Black Walnut glanced at each other. They knew what the summons meant. The glance they shared also conveyed mutual shock. Neither had considered such a possibility, and they certainly had never discussed it. Black Walnut shrugged before looking away from his wife, and dutifully followed Wanders Far to the council hut. Black Walnut's three sons followed as far as the entrance.

Corn stood dumbfounded for several minutes. She didn't know what to do, but she felt like she should be doing something. Finally, she grabbed the baby and went outside. She wished she was at the council, watching Black Walnut's interview. Then she thought it would be too nerve-wracking and was glad she was not at the council watching the interview. Her heart raced. What if Black Walnut did become chief? What would she do? She hadn't ever thought to observe what the chief's wife did. Finally, she went back into her longhouse, and found her grandmother, Gentle Breeze. Gentle Breeze held Corn's hands and looked deep into her eyes as her granddaughter talked. Corn told Gentle Breeze about what had happened and confessed her insecurities.

Gentle Breeze could easily relate. Gentle Breeze was the oldest woman in her house. She had long ago ceded the head of household responsibilities to her oldest daughter, Bear Fat. Gentle Breeze was thoughtful, hardworking, and nurturing, but took no interest in governing the house and the village. In addition to being thoughtful, hardworking, and nurturing, Bear Fat was also willing to make decisions affecting the families in the longhouse, and to sit at council with the women in charge of the other longhouses in the village. They were responsible for the governance of the village. When it came time to make such decisions, they chose the chief, they set the rules, and they passed judgements whenever grievances occurred. After ten years on the council, Bear Fat was named matriarch, and had chaired the Women's Council ever since. Though she herself had abdicated, Gentle Breeze advised Corn, "Don't worry, things will work out the way they were meant to, and if your family is called to serve, you will find it within you."

Corn protested. "I'm not so sure. I might need a lot of help. What does a chief's wife do?" Corn listened intently while Gentle Breeze explained the duties of a chief's wife from her perspective. Corn thought of her father, Big Canoe, and the role he played, supporting his wife as she served as the village's matriarch.

Finally, Black Walnut returned to the longhouse, and found Corn in the first compartment, closest to the door. He sat by the fire, put his arm around Corn, and nodded at Gentle Breeze. They listened intently as he told them about the interview, the questions they asked, and the answers he gave. When he finished, Corn turned her head, furrowed her brow, and asked, "What if they pick you?"

Black Walnut said, "If called, I will serve, of course. But how could they pick me when there are other, far more qualified, brave and wise men who could be chief?"

Instantly, Corn's outlook flipped. "Who is braver? Who is wiser? Who is more qualified? I can't think of anybody who could do a better job than you!" Corn's defense was so intense that by the end of it she realized she was yelling and lowered her voice to a whisper. "Oh well, whatever happens, I love you. We shall have to wait and see."

The women voted again the next morning. Each woman voted for only one man. It was a tie. 10 to 10 to 0, so they were down to two finalists. Bear Fat suggested, "Go out and spend the rest of the day talking about these two men in our village. Remember that we are talking about naming a man to lead the men when they are outside of the village, and we are naming a man to be responsible for the safety of our village. We are not looking for that man which we women find the most agreeable."

The results were clear. The following morning, after listening to Bear Fat's guidance, and talking with the people in the village, the women's vote was eighteen to two. After that vote had been revealed,

Bear Fat asked if they could leave the council with a unanimous decision.

The women exited the council hut and stood by the central fire until, slowly, everyone in the village joined them. Wanders Far had been sent to run through every longhouse and call everyone to the fire.

Bear Fat began speaking in a cheerful tone. "The women have chosen our new chief. Our village is lucky to have great men, great warriors, and we are thriving here at Garoga Creek. We were well-served by our departed chief, and we will miss him. Yes, the mourning period has ended, but still we mourn. We must now look to the future. Our people must be protected, and our men must be well led. We carefully considered every option, which is to say every man in the village, from young to old. Then we rounded our choice down to three men. We would have been well served to choose the most experienced man who has been so valuable to us for so many years. We would have been well served to choose the best planner, who our men depend on so greatly. Instead, we have chosen a leader so powerful, he hasn't even realized and appreciated the leadership skills he possesses. He has been responsible for teaching our young men everything they need to do to succeed, and to protect us. We have chosen a man who could be chief for generations. The Women's Council has unanimously decided to name Black Walnut the chief of the Bear Clan."

Initially, the crowd was stunned. There was silence. Then, clapping, shouting, and chanting sounds filled the air. The announcement immediately turned into a celebration. Drummers ran to get their instruments. The village celebrated all afternoon, throughout the evening and well into the night.

When the party was over, Black Walnut and Corn returned to their longhouse, and climbed into their bunk, exhausted. Corn turned to her husband and said, "Now what do we do?"

"I don't know," Black Walnut chuckled quietly, trying not to wake the kids above them. "Nobody told me how to be a chief," he continued. A moment later, he concluded, "I'm sure your mother will tell me what to do in the morning." They laughed and snuggled in under their blankets.

Chapter Ten
Attacked at Dawn

B y the time Wanders Far was 8-years-old, his family had completely given up trying to keep track of him. Their friends and family had grown tired of endlessly having to search the village every time the boy wandered down a game trail. Since it had proven impossible to teach him to communicate his whereabouts, or trying to assign people to watch him, Bear Fat and Big Canoe prepared the boy with the knowledge he would need to survive in the wilds of the woods, even if he wandered into them with no prior preparation.

That training came in useful the summer after his brother Chipmunk joined his new wife's village among the Oneida, which was about sixty-five miles directly to the west.

One morning that summer, Wanders Far thought about his brother, and wondered whether Chipmunk missed his family. There was one way to know for sure, he thought. Then he visualized the way to get there. His whole family had made the trip twice the year before. Early that spring, they had traveled to help distant relatives in that village build some new longhouses. His brother Chipmunk loved building the structures; in particular he enjoyed working on the roofs. He seemed to be at his happiest, scampering around on the roof. At their own longhouse on Garoga Creek, Chipmunk spent most of his time on his perch on the roof where he loved to look out over the meandering creek in the valley at the bottom of the hill. If someone inquired, he would reassure them that he was keeping watch.

Whenever Chipmunk would pause to take a break from his work in the Oneida village, he noticed a young lady on the ground watching him. It made him happy whenever he thought of her, and he felt like his heart raced whenever he saw her down below. She had made it a point to be within sight of him at every opportunity. By the time the new longhouses were finished, they had become quite smitten with one another. Summer separated them, but after Chipmunk returned from his annual summer hunting trip with his family, they were married late in the fall. He hadn't seen anybody from his birth village for three seasons, until that day Wanders Far suddenly appeared in the village.

It was remarkable for a boy as young as Wanders Far to have such a keen sense of direction, and to remember the way to get from one place to another. The paths between the various villages along the way were worn well enough to be followed, particularly by someone who knew how to read them. Wanders Far also possessed a photographic memory, at least when it came to the woodlands, forests, streams, and fields. He could remember the slightest difference between rocks or trees that looked the same to others.

When it occurred to Wanders Far to make the trip, he started off down the trail. He hadn't decided to go, but he thought he might. He figured if he did decide to go, he would already be part way there. If he decided not to go, he would just turn back. The miles passed quickly and easily beneath his feet. He could easily walk all day without complaint. He was a small boy. Despite the constant pestering of his loving grandmother, he rarely ate more than a few bites of food at a time. Along the path, he stopped several times, pausing to enjoy some delicious Mayapples. Though he didn't enjoy them, he dug up a few wild leeks to eat when his stomach growled at him. Wild strawberries were plentiful and within close proximity to his path, and it was the peak of their season. Wanders Far never needed to contemplate using the knife tied to his shin or the bola tied at his waist. He had plenty to eat, and there was plenty of water along the way.

Strange thoughts, like tiny dreams, appeared in his mind as he walked. The dreams lasted no more than several seconds. He saw a building made of sand colored blocks on the top of a mountain. The building was bigger than a hundred longhouses put together. He had never seen anything like it in his life, and yet he felt like he knew that place just the same. He wondered if it was possible that somehow he had been there before. It was something to think about as the miles went by.

He made it thirty-five miles the first day and found a tiny abandoned hut on the bank of a small pond along the path. It provided the perfect opportunity for him to sleep safely through the night. He had thought about how he would set up a camp, using one of the many methods his parents had taught him. It would be an easy night, and he would be back on the trail early the next morning. It never occurred to him to be afraid, and he slept soundly.

Most of the next day was uneventful. He walked as if he hadn't a care in the world, humming happily to himself as the miles went by. He figured he was getting close, recalling a large boulder from the previous year. He figured he had maybe five more miles to go. Beyond the boulder was a stream. Something by the stream caught his eye. He stopped dead in his tracks. Very slowly, he squatted down, with his hands on his knees, looking out over the tops of the tall grass. There was a party of ten full-grown men. Their heads and chests were painted blue. A dark, blackish sort of blue. Algonquin!

Wanders Far thought about the stories he had been told. Those men had to be Algonquin. Where were they headed? His heart sank. He had a hunch. A very strong feeling told him that the war party was headed toward his brother's village. Fortunately, they didn't seem to be in any hurry. They didn't notice the small boy crouched on the trail.

Fearfully, he tiptoed down the trail, past the war party, careful not to make a sound. His heart beat so frantically, he worried that the enemy could hear it thumping too. When he was sure it was safe, he took off running. An hour later, he reached the entrance to the palisade at the village and ran straight into his brother, Chipmunk, who was shocked to see his baby brother standing there alone, winded, sixty-five miles from his home.

Despite being short of breath, Wanders Far blurted out the news of what he had seen by the river an hour's run to the east. Chipmunk took his brother to see the chief of his village, and Wanders Far repeated the news, spitting the words out as fast as he possibly could, as if the war party had been in hot pursuit. The chief sent out a half dozen scouts, armed with the information he had received from the kid, and then he told Wanders Far that he was a hero. The chief invited Wanders Far to a special dinner in his honor that night. Of course, his brother Chipmunk and his wife were invited too.

At dinner they learned from the scouts that the Algonquin party had been sighted and had moved to a distance far closer than when Wanders Far had seen them. At dusk they had been seen preparing a fireless camp less than half a mile away. The people of Chipmunk's village prepared to be attacked at dawn.

Every man in the village was awake at three in the morning. One party of ten men took up protected positions to the north of the route the Algonquins were expected to use for an approach, and another ten men took up positions to the south.

As the light of the first rays of sun peeked over the eastern horizon, the Algonquins quickly and quietly sped along a direct path from their encampment toward the Oneida's village, hoping they could surprise the encampment and make off with some valuable goods and perhaps a scalp or two before being run off. Or maybe they could burn the village and weaken their enemies.

The enemy didn't get close enough to the Oneida village to land an arrow in the palisades that surrounded it. All at once, ten arrows flew at them from the north. Three Algonquins fell dead in their tracks. Before they could fully comprehend that their surprise attack was not a surprise, ten more arrows flew in from the south. A fourth Algonquin fell dead on the trail. The remaining Algonquins bolted back down the path. Fortunate for them, they were very fast runners. The Oneidas followed in quick pursuit and didn't return home until they were able to report that the enemy was at least twenty-five miles to the north.

Wanders Far attended another hero's feast at the chief's longhouse. The four dead Algonquin were on display. He stared at the dead men for a long time. Then he closed his eyes and pictured them at home with their families, families just like his own, and wondered why they had to come to attack the Oneida village. He hoped that the Oneida had been fierce enough to make the retreating Algonquins think twice about making another attempt.

The next day, Wanders Far was ready to start back down the trail toward his home village. Privately, the chief inquired of Chipmunk as to whether Wanders Far should return down the path alone. Chipmunk explained, though he was extremely young, that he had a free spirit. He was well-trained, and though he was only 8-years-old, his family had no choice but to hope for the best. No village would hold him. He was a runner.

Wanders Far would return home to a family most relieved to see him, safe and sound, and amazed to hear the story of the raid on the Oneidas. He also delivered tears of joy to his mother and grandmother, who were happy to learn that Chipmunk's wife was due to have a baby, perhaps any day.

Tears were streaming down Bear Fat's face, happy with the news of another grandchild, and grateful for the safe return of her youngest boy. She bent down, cupped his cheeks in her hands, kissed his forehead, and then, with her face six inches from his face, eyes locked with his, she said gently, "Wanders Far, could you tell me when you are making a long journey? I'll still worry, but I will worry less when I know you're gone on purpose." Bear Fat couldn't think of any other 8-year-old whose parents would allow their son to be away from their village on overnight solo excursions. She knew her boy was not an ordinary 8-year-old, and she knew that he was following the path he was meant to follow. Every day she thought about her lost baby girl. Missing Blackberry and worrying about Wanders Far at the same time always gave her a sick feeling in the pit of her stomach.

Wanders Far tucked his chin to his chest and apologized, but as soon as the very next morning, he forgot to tell his mother where he was headed. His feet led him down the trail toward the Wolf Clan village to share the news of his visit to the Oneida village. His oldest brother, Fisher, didn't know that Chipmunk was also going to be a father.

Chapter Eleven
An Algonquin Captive

Early autumn the following year, a hunting party returned from the north with an Algonquin captive. The enemy scout had become separated from a party of warriors and unwittingly crossed paths with the hunting party. The scout was unable to steal away, undetected. In addition to their captive, the hunters also returned with a fat elk, three deer, seven turkeys, and a partridge.

As they approached the village, the captive was made to strip. They led him to a raised platform just outside of the council house. The platform stood three feet from the ground. The prisoner was tied, spread-eagled to posts at his wrists and ankles. He sang loudly, bravely, and defiantly in his own language, the story of his short life.

The leader of the Bear Clan's hunting party savagely bit down on the fingernail of the captive's left index finger with his molars, and violently shook his head and jaw until the finger nail was fully removed. He spat the nail on the platform at the feet of the captive, who sneered and spat in the face of his enemy. The captive received a sharp slap on his right cheek from the hand of his enemy. Then the captor gestured with his hand and arm, as if welcoming the entire village to join him on the small platform, which they lined up to do one at a time.

The captive started his song again and sang it as loudly as he could. Each of the villagers struck him with a stick. The captive was taunted mercilessly. Each villager brought a new insult. Every aspect of the captive's appearance was mocked, especially his genitals, which he had painted the same dark blue as his head. The captive met the gaze of each of his attackers. His eyelids were painted crimson and accentuated his demonic appearance. A black lightning bolt on his right cheek added to the ferocious impression he portrayed. He was about a head taller than most of his captors, strong, and slender. Nonetheless, it was plain to see the captive was a very young man, barely more than a boy. He had been taught well by his people.

Gentle Breeze was the last in line. In her many years, she had witnessed that ritual dozens of times. It never became easier. Every time the captive was stricken, she winced. She knew better than to protest. As a child she had been sharply rebuked for asking for mercy for one of their captives, and in that instance, the captive was beaten more harshly.

She climbed the steps to the platform carrying her stick. She carefully inspected the captive. As she looked at him from each angle, she looked back and forth to the lead hunter. She poked him several different places with the end of her stick, grunting approval or disapproval with each motion. Finally, she whacked his behind with her stick, turned to the lead hunter, and asked whether he would sell her the captive. The bargain was made at the price of a canoe. She no longer needed Red-Winged Blackbird's canoe anyway. The captive was untied from the pole. Gentle Breeze took the captive by the hand, and proclaimed to her fellow villagers, "He'll make a fine new husband! Meet Blue Arrow," she laughed as she motioned toward his groin. The crowd erupted with laughter and cheers. Then she surprised her new husband with a quick closed-mouthed kiss on the lips and led him to her longhouse.

Bear Fat and her family stood there in the darkness, shocked. Bear Fat shook her head back and forth and followed her mother to the entrance of their longhouse. Though she never expected it, Bear Fat knew exactly what her mother did, and why she did it. Bear Fat thought the acting was very good, but she wondered whether her mother had thought through the implications.

The surprised captive was quickly invited to sit at their hearth fire. The family sat down around the fire as Gentle Breeze brought blankets, a bowl of stew, and some cornbread to Blue Arrow. She sprinkled some dried strawberries on top of the cornbread. After he was fed, Gentle Breeze served the rest of the family. Because Gentle Breeze declared the captive as a replacement relative, he was treated like family, as custom dictated. It was just as common for captives to become tortured slaves—sometimes killed for entertainment value, and sometimes returned to their people, barely alive. Blue Arrow was lucky, and they all knew it but it was never discussed between and among them, then or in the years that followed.

After dinner, Bear Fat suggested that Big Canoe, Dandelion, and Wanders Far take Blue Arrow down to the dammed pond in the creek. Blue Arrow was with his new family, and no longer needed to wear the colors of a warrior headed to battle. He knew what custom dictated. He understood that he had become a full member of a family that was brand new to him. He thought briefly, they were strangely foreign and familiar at the same time. He didn't dwell on thoughts for long. He knew the role he was expected to play, and that required all of his attention. No time for idle thoughts.

When they returned to the hearth fire, the family was startled to see just how young Blue Arrow was, perhaps 14-years-old. In his fierce paint, he had looked a couple of years older. Gentle Breeze washed the dried blood from his finger, applied a salve, and wrapped it in leaves, bound together with a firmly tied string. Meanwhile, Big Canoe told Blue Arrow about Gentle Breeze's husband who had died ten years earlier. Then he told a brief story about each member of the family, and the story of how he and Bear Fat met and married.

It didn't take long. Big Canoe was a man of few words. A good, decent, friendly man, but not much of a storyteller.

When he was done, Bear Fat asked Blue Arrow to tell his story. Dandelion added, "Yes, Grandfather, tell us a story!" Everyone, including Blue Arrow, laughed at Dandelion's good-hearted joke, however from that moment on, both Dandelion and Wanders Far called Blue Arrow by the name Grandfather. Dandelion's humor and storytelling helped everyone to become more comfortable with the sudden, seemingly permanent change brought upon the family.

Gentle Breeze brought a little bowl of bear grease, lathered her fingers with it, and ran her hands through Blue Arrow's hair. Six months earlier, Blue Arrow's mother had greased his hair for him. It crossed his mind for an instant—Gentle Breeze is now my wife, not my mother or grandmother. He quickly forced those thoughts from his mind. Everyone was looking at him expectantly. He began to speak.

It was late when Blue Arrow finished telling his boyhood story to his new family. Gentle Breeze put him to bed in the bunk above her own, just as she had put her children to bed years before. She climbed several steps up the ladder, kissed his forehead, and climbed back down the ladder to her own bunk. As she drifted off to sleep, pleased with herself, Gentle Breeze wondered whether she had saved Blue Arrow's life. She was happy either way, whether she had saved his life or merely prevented the suffering he would have received as a slave.

Blue Arrow lay in the bunk, thinking about all that had happened that day. As he recalled bravely facing his tormentors, he smiled proudly. He had been prepared for such a moment. His Algonquin father, grandfather, uncles, brothers, and cousins had told him what he must do if he were faced with such a situation. They would be proud, he thought. He thought of his family back home and knew they would be worried. A tear fell from the corner of his eye. He quickly wiped it away with his thumb. He thought of the old woman in the bunk beneath him. To think she had parted with a canoe to save him. Yes, he had been brave, and he had prepared himself to face his death that day. Blue Arrow felt deeply grateful, and happy to be in the company of such a wonderful family. He thought of his mother, and his family back home, and wondered if he would see them again. Though he was tired, with all that had happened that day, Blue Arrow could not fall asleep.

In the middle of the night, Blue Arrow climbed down from the bunk above, slipped beneath the thick black bearskin blanket and joined Gentle Breeze. He whispered in her ear, "I am your husband, not your child." A fact he quickly demonstrated.

Blue Arrow remained in the village for several months. He became well loved by all, including the hunters who had captured him. Most of his time was spent with Dandelion and Wanders Far. Despite their unusual relationship, and despite being raised in enemy tribes, they acted like brothers raised together from birth. They connected from the first day, as if they knew each other already. As custom dictated, Gentle Breeze accepted Blue Arrow as her husband at night. When she closed her eyes tightly, she felt young and she felt the presence of Red-Winged Blackbird. Sometimes Gentle Breeze briefly admonished herself for putting them in such a strange situation. It never took her long to get back to feeling righteous. She loved Blue Arrow like a grandson. She was glad she saved him. She tried for months, but she couldn't accept him in her heart as a husband.

A couple of months went by, and early fall gave way to late autumn. A couple of weeks after the first frost, the family was gathered for dinner. Gentle Breeze had prepared a spectacular feast. Bear Fat inquired, "Are we celebrating something, Mother?"

Gentle Breeze said, "Yes. I have been thinking long and hard. We have enjoyed the company of Blue Arrow here for more than two moons. Already we love him, just as if he had spent his whole life with us, but I think we all know he belongs with his own people to the north. He deserves a young wife who can give him fine sons and daughters. I will miss him every day of my life. I think he should return home before the rivers freeze. I think you should take him tomorrow. Dandelion, Wanders Far, would you do this for me?"

The family mumbled in agreement. Blue Arrow cocked his head left, then right, as if debating in his own head. He hadn't considered such an outcome. Always eager to prove himself a man, Blue Arrow thought to firmly assert his own opinion. However, he couldn't think of what that opinion should be. In the face of his indecision, the family begrudgingly proceeded to accept Gentle Breeze's plan.

Gentle Breeze nudged the family mood and said, "This is meant to be a celebration dinner. We honor our beloved Blue Arrow, and we beg him to remember us kindly and with love." She smiled widely, tilted her head toward her right shoulder. Tears streaming down her face, she added, "I love you, Blue Arrow." He stood, and they shared a long hug. After a minute or two, the rest of the family stood as well, and piled in for a giant group hug. Wanders Far couldn't bring himself to participate. He silently stepped sideways through the doorway. He needed some time to himself.

The next morning, Dandelion, Wanders Far, and Blue Arrow set out from the village wearing warm skins, carrying heavy packs, and a medium sized canoe. The journey began with a long twenty-mile hike to the Sacandaga River, known as the River of the Drowned Lands because it meandered through seemingly endless swamps.

The travelers were not in a mood to rush their journey. They enjoyed having a few last days together before they would have to say farewell. Although there were several hours of daylight remaining, they leisurely worked to make camp for the evening. Though they should have gone to sleep when the sun set, they told stories, shared dreams, and laughed well into the evening. Nonetheless, they were hard at work breaking camp at first light.

It was a clear and chilly morning. An icy frost clung to the banks of the river. The icy fronds on top of the tall grasses reflected the early rays of the morning sun and began to melt. The dark brown heads of cattails were sparsely coated with frost. The result was a speckled and mottled brown and white pattern.

They put the canoe in the swampy river and began paddling in a northeast direction. It was one of those days that seemed to require silence and reverence. They quietly dipped their paddles in the water, slowly and deliberately, minimizing the disturbance created by their passage through the silent swamp. Wanders Far whispered, "Such a perfect morning must please the Great Spirit immensely and must not be violated."

A mile into the journey, they saw an enormous bull moose. He stood in the swamp, motionless, as if enjoying the reflection of his huge antlers on the surface of the still water. He did not seem disturbed by their proximity, though they came within thirty feet of him. They could have easily filled him full of arrows.

A couple of miles later, a beaver's dam came into view. "Look, Grandfather," Wanders Far said to Blue Arrow, pointing to the mound of sticks and twigs. They paddled closer. The peaceful quiet of that morning was disturbed by a young beaver's frolicking morning swim. Just for the fun of it, the animal darted in one direction, then another. As they got closer, the beaver swam up to the canoe, then around it. Evidently, he didn't have the good sense to be afraid of people in a canoe. They paddled on, and three other beavers poked their noses above the surface of the seemingly endless swamp.

They reached the confluence of rivers a couple of hours before dark. They had a crackling fire going quickly, and soon after that they enjoyed a warm fish soup. They carried baskets full of Gentle Breeze's delicious cornbread, enough to last a month. Some was meant to be shared with Blue Arrow's family as a gift to celebrate their reunification. The three travelers enjoyed a little cornbread that evening.

Blue Arrow asked his companions if they were nervous to meet his family and his people. Wanders Far was apprehensive about meeting the enemy of his tribe, but instead said, "Nervous? No, Dandelion here could charm the spots off a bobcat cub!"

Dandelion laughed, "Good one, Brother. Let me try. I'm so smooth, I could charm the quills from a porcupine's hump. Oh… or, how about this: I'm so captivating I could charm the rattle off a snake's tail!"

Blue Arrow added, "My turn! My Grandson here is so suave, he could charm the armor off a sturgeon or the whiskers from a catfish."

Wanders Far added, "Not to mention the trail of fainting girls' bodies when Dandelion walks through neighboring villages." Dandelion pounded his chest, shrugged, and laughed. He couldn't explain it himself, but his brother was right on that score.

They continued to shoot the breeze, entertaining each other with foolish stories and ridiculous notions late into the night before falling asleep.

In the morning they started up the North River. They maintained a faster pace. By mid-afternoon they reached the point at which the river became shallow, then turned back in a southerly direction before turning to the west. At that shallow point, they pulled the canoe from the river and hid it under a pile of leaves so that Dandelion and Wanders Far could use it again on the return trip. Then they set out on foot, due north a couple of miles through dense woodlands and set up camp for their last evening together at Bird Pond. Several nights of staying up late and a vigorous day of paddling and hiking left them less inclined to stay up late. All three travelers were asleep within minutes after they closed their eyes.

A light snow fell overnight. In the morning, they hastily shook the snow off their furs and packed their baskets for their final ten-mile march. The trees surrounding the circumference of Bird Pond looked perfect: pristine, clean, and white with their fresh coat of light snow.

By mid-day the snow was gone, and it was rapidly becoming unseasonably warm. Most of the deciduous trees had lost hold of their brightly colored leaves. Blue Arrow's village wasn't far. They began to hear the distant sound of voices. They walked on and reached a small clearing with a large rock in a small field of short grass. Blue Arrow raised his hand, signaling that his companions should stop and wait.

Ten minutes later, Dandelion and Wanders Far heard a loud, thunderous roar of welcome from Blue Arrow's village. His people were surprised and overwhelmed by his unexpected return after being missing almost ten weeks.

Blue Arrow returned to the clearing about twenty minutes later, and they were warmly greeted by Blue Arrow's small band of Algonquins. There were thirty people, and almost all of them were directly related to Blue Arrow, one way or another. Their little village was set up outside the mouth of a big cave.

The village consisted of eight wickiups. They were seven feet tall with a diameter of twelve feet. The wickiups were placed in a circle and their entrances faced each other. At the middle of the village was a communal hearth.

Everyone gathered around the fire in the middle of the village, and half a dozen women quickly began preparing a feast. Meanwhile, Blue Arrow introduced Wanders Far and then Dandelion as his new grandsons. Everyone looked at each other with quizzical looks. Had Blue Arrow gone mad? Blue Arrow asked Dandelion if he could tell everyone what had happened since Blue Arrow had disappeared.

Dandelion was happy to oblige. Mostly he stuck to the facts and presented them chronologically. He recognized that his audience was in no hurry, so he included plenty of detail. In deference to the unknown customs of his hosts, he held back when he might otherwise have added dramatic or comedic flair.

Wanders Far watched the faces of the Algonquins as they listened to his brother Dandelion tell Blue Arrow's new story. In particular he watched Blue Arrow's mother. He tried to lock every detail he could into his memory so that he could picture that day again in the future.

Blue Arrow's grandfather was wrapped in a large woven blanket over his shoulders and a smaller, matching blanket covered his head, hanging well over his forehead and casting a long shadow across his face. The old man never spoke and barely moved. Though Wanders Far couldn't see more than his earlobes, cheeks, and chin, he was intrigued. There was something about the man that made Wanders Far wonder. It occurred to Wanders Far that their paths would cross again.

The entrance to the cave was enormous and shaped like an eye. After the feast and celebration, Blue Arrow took his companions on a tour of the giant cave and told the story of how his family had to slaughter a large family of bears to take over the cave. A river flowed almost to the mouth of the cave, then disappeared underground. Inside the cave, the river flowed like an indoor waterfall. In another section of the cave was a small lake. Blue Arrow claimed the water was good for drinking and good for swimming, though it was far too cold to swim so late in the season.

After dinner, Dandelion entertained his hosts with some of his favorite stories about his family and his village. As it got later, people said goodnight and headed for their wickiups. Too soon it was nearing midnight and only Dandelion, Wanders Far, and Blue Arrow remained at the fire. They shared their parting thoughts that evening. Blue Arrow was welcome to return and visit at Garoga Creek any time. They also told Blue Arrow how to find them in the summertime at Copperas Pond. They promised they would never forget each other.

As Wanders Far was falling asleep, he thought about Blue Arrow. He had been with the family only ten weeks, but it already felt like he was losing a brother. He knew Dandelion felt the same way. Wanders Far finally fell asleep, having failed to console himself about their coming separation.

In the morning there were no words. Dandelion and Wanders Far waved to their hosts, and headed back the way they came, in a hurry to get home before the first major snowstorm of the season arrived.

Wanders Far concentrated to see if he could picture a future time together with Dandelion and Blue Arrow. It didn't come to him. Disappointed, he hung his head. He could not conjure up a vision. The rest of the way home they moved fast, and said little, mourning the loss of someone, though he hadn't died.

Chapter Twelve
Utopia

Bear Fat was unusually excited. She couldn't wait to share the experience of summer in the mountains with her mother. For years they had talked about bringing her, and for years there always seemed to be a reason she needed to stay behind in the village. Every year when Bear Fat and her family would return, telling stories of the summer, Gentle Breeze would listen, entranced, and wistfully wish she could go too. Then every spring, something always seemed to prevent her from joining her family.

They had to hike to the primary waterway. Gentle Breeze was a physically fit, 61-year-old great-grandmother, and she kept a decent pace. Wanders Far and Dandelion led the procession up the trail, followed by Bear Fat, then Gentle Breeze. Big Canoe brought up the rear. They weren't in a big hurry and stopped whenever someone thought a break might be nice. In past years, the family had made the hundred-mile trek in four days. Nobody minded the slower pace, and they spent six nights on the way to Moose River.

Near the river bank, there were two canoes hidden in a thicket, a short distance from the established path, just where they had been left at the end of the previous summer. The boys took the smaller canoe, Dandelion in the stern, and Wanders Far at the bow. Dandelion had a strong chest and muscular arms, whereas Wanders Far had strong legs, but not much upper body strength. It was difficult for them to synchronize to a comfortable pace, but that made it easier for the second canoe to keep up with the first. Big Canoe took the stern of the large canoe and Bear Fat paddled from the front. Gentle Breeze and most of the gear rode in the middle.

A series of rivers, ponds, and lakes took them most of the distance from south to north. They could have summered anywhere along the way and found a bounty of resources. Other, shorter mountains had plenty of bear, deer, trout, and birch trees, but tradition prevented anybody in the family from considering or suggesting going anywhere other than Copperas Pond. It was nice to look at other places along the way, but there was no place else they wanted to be, most of the time. Copperas Pond was their utopia.

Gentle Breeze enjoyed every second of the trip, soaking in the beauty of the scenery along the way, gazing off into the woods with wide-eyed wonderment. Whenever she could, she would reach over the edge of the canoe and drag her hand or feet in the water. Big Canoe and Bear Fat shifted their balance to compensate and prevent the canoe from flipping over as Gentle Breeze flopped about. Every time Gentle Breeze would say something like, "Oh my," or "look, look, look," Big Canoe and Bear Fat would exchange a glance and a grin. It was like they were seeing everything along the way for the first time, too. In all her years, Gentle Breeze had rarely left her village, spending most of her time within the palisade walls.

After a fairly leisurely five days and ninety miles of paddling, they reached the end of their waterway. They set up camp along a medium-sized lake and hid the canoes in their customary hiding place. The next morning, they put the packs back on their backs and hiked the final fifteen miles to their summer residence.

Their camp was exactly how they had left it the previous fall. It was a much smaller version of their Garoga Creek longhouse, with plenty of room for two families. They had rebuilt the camp two summers previous. It was sturdy and tightly enclosed. They were glad not to find raccoons, opossums, skunks, or other nuisance animals residing in their shelter. Gentle Breeze squealed with delight when she saw it. "How cute," she raved. Though it was pretty tidy, she set to cleaning the house with a pine bough, then she cleaned the outdoor area between the house and a fire pit, just like she did at home in their village. Big Canoe and the boys gathered wood, twigs, and bark. It wasn't long before Bear Fat had a small fire on a bed of dried moss. It felt warm against her skin. She added larger twigs, then more substantial chopped logs they had left behind at the end of the previous summer. When that fire was established, Bear Fat started another, smaller fire in the hearth inside, at the center of the tiny house, just enough so that the fire would keep them comfortable in bearskin robes on their bunks.

Back at the bigger fire outdoors, Bear Fat set up a large clay pot, filled it with stream water, and provisions from the parfleche pouches she brought with her to make a stew. She added some tallow to make the stew hearty.

When there was more than enough wood, twigs, and branches to last several weeks, they all gathered around the fire, happy to be facing each other after days of sitting single file in canoes. The hot meal was pleasant, and there was plenty of it. They laughed, talked, and made plans. After wintering in a house with fifty people, they enjoyed the intimate solitude and warmth of their time together at camp. There was a lot of work to do in the summer to provide for their enormously extended family during the winter, yet summer at the camp on the little pond provided leisure and relaxation as well. Gentle Breeze was overcome with emotion, tears in her eyes, radiating gratitude for the opportunity to experience summer with her oldest daughter's family.

Wasting no time, the next morning Big Canoe and Dandelion set out in pursuit of bears. They carried weapons and sufficient provisions to be gone a week. It usually didn't take that long. Big Canoe knew exactly where to look after a lifetime of experience.

Copperas Pond was situated at the foot of an enormous mountain. Sometimes even in the summer, the top of the mountain would have snow, and often, even on cloudless days, the very top of the mountain would be lost within a cloud. Big Canoe knew all the nooks, crannies, and rocky outcrops on the mountain, and they trekked from one to the other until they found an area they liked.

Back at camp, Bear Fat got everything ready for the work that would come. She prepared racks for drying meat at the fire and got stakes ready for stretching the hides. When the hides were stretched taut, she would have work to do, scraping and curing them for use by her family, or for trading for other things they would need. There were hundreds of tasks to tend to at camp, and she scurried around, humming, and every once in a while, inhaling the scent of the nearby cedars.

Wanders Far kept his grandmother busy, showing her everything there was to see. He taught her how to catch fish in the nearby river, which seemed to delight her. Whenever she caught a fish, she seemed so surprised, it was as if she thought there was no chance of actually catching a fish. Yet one after another, she pulled them in, giggling when they flopped in her hands, as if the fish were intentionally tickling her palms. She kept Wanders Far busy, removing the fish from the bone hooks on her string, and knocking them on the head with a rock.

On one side of Copperas Pond was a ledge, twenty feet above the water's surface. Jumping into the pond from the ledge was an exhilarating feeling, and almost as much fun for the adults as for the children. Gentle Breeze watched Wanders Far jump in a couple of times. Whenever he jumped, she felt a dropping, sinking feeling in the pit of her stomach, almost as if she were jumping herself. Every time he got out of the pond, dripping wet, she praised him. "Nice jump," or "good job," she would say. Then she made the mistake of saying, "I wish I could do that!"

Wanders Far took her by the hand and led her up the trail to the top ledge rock. "It really isn't a big jump," he assured her. "You can do this. You are a great swimmer, and I'm here for you," he added, as if he were an adult, and she were a little girl.

Gentle Breeze giggled. She was amused by her grandson. She thought, since I've been here, I actually feel like a little girl again. She had no complaints about her own childhood, but on the other hand, she hadn't known what she was missing. She said to her grandson, "You know what, yes! I think I will. I am going to do it. You think I can? All I have to do is jump, and then swim for the top once I land in the water?" It took her several minutes to tiptoe up to the edge. Then she leaned forward slightly, and peeked over the slightly rounded, convex rock beneath her. It took five seconds and one massive push from her grandson to send her flying out over the edge. Her arms and legs flailed as she went over the edge, and she gulped for breath before she hit the surface.

Bear Fat watched from camp where she was busy fashioning a new basket. She thought her mother would go up with Wanders Far, and watch *him* jump from there, then walk back down the path. She never expected *her* to jump, and she never expected Wanders Far to push her. It was so unlike him to do such a thing. If she hadn't seen it for herself, she wouldn't have believed it. Perhaps what made it seem so funny was how unexpected it was. She was doubled over with laughter as her mother got out of the pond, dripping wet, and jumping up and down with excitement.

"I know," Bear Fat hollered to her mother from across the pond, "refreshing, isn't it?"

Wanders Far was right behind her. He couldn't wait to congratulate her on her big jump. Bear Fat thought that she should admonish her son for pushing his grandmother off a cliff, but just the thought of scolding him set her off into another fit of laughter. Before she was done, her mother was back up the trail, on her way to the edge of the cliff again. No hesitation the second time, she jumped right in as if she'd done it hundreds of times. Every time she jumped in that summer, she giggled and radiated just the same as she did after her first trip over the edge.

Another day that summer, Wanders Far took Gentle Breeze on a tour of all the little ponds in the area. There were four all together. Each one was a little different, and each was beautiful in its own way. Then one day, he took her on a hike to a good-sized brook. They went around a bend, and there was a waterfall, coming over the edge of a square rock so that the water fell evenly, in a uniform spray. The height was twenty feet from the bottom to the top. They swam in the pool beneath the waterfall. Then he showed her how to go through the water and sit behind it. When they made it to the cavity just behind the waterfall, she put her hands over her mouth in amazement, as if she could bottle the excitement up inside her. "What a special place," she exclaimed. Then Wanders Far showed her how to sit just right underneath it so that the water from above would hit her shoulders, making for an invigorating massage. Then, sitting forward, the water hit the small of her back, and Gentle Breeze said, "Wow, that's just what I needed. I love this place!"

On the way back to the pond, they saw a big doe grazing near the path. "Don't move," Wanders Far whispered to his grandmother. Neither of them moved, not one muscle. Not even to blink their eyes. As long as they stood perfectly still, the deer didn't notice their presence. The doe wandered closely. Surprisingly close. Gentle Breeze thought she could reach out and pet the deer, and she really wanted to. The closest the deer got was fifteen feet away. Gentle Breeze thought she had locked eyes with the deer and could see into her soul. She admired its long eyelashes and dark oval eyes. A fly landed on the tip of Gentle Breeze's nose, and she wiggled her nose to send the fly off. It was just enough movement to send the deer into a panic. She darted off into the woods, bouncing, almost as if she were flying. A clump of mud flew up from the hoof of the deer and landed on the tip of Gentle Breeze's nose where the fly had been. She and Wanders Far laughed until they cried. Gentle Breeze forgot to wash the mud off her nose, which made the story that much funnier when they got back to the pond and shared it with Bear Fat.

That summer was full of joy and wonder, and made for memories the whole family would cherish. Most evenings around the campfire, they would laugh, tell stories, and remember previous trips. Dandelion in particular liked to tell all the family's stories, even the ones that were from way before his time. Gentle Breeze enjoyed hearing them. Though she had heard them before, it was different to hear all the stories about the family's summer in the mountains while she was there herself.

While Dandelion was telling stories about his older sisters' trips to the mountains many years earlier, Bear Fat started thinking about her son the storyteller. He was a strong, good looking young man, extremely personable, and a skilled craftsman, having perfected the art of making canoes. Big Canoe and Dandelion enjoyed spending as much time together as they could. Dandelion hadn't displayed any urgency for any other task except for hunting bears, making canoes, and enjoying the company of friends. Bear Fat thought about how the fluff of a dandelion blew in the wind without any thought to where it was going, which was why she had called him Dandelion since he was a young boy. Carefree.

Most family conversations began with something Dandelion would say, and most conversations were continued because of what Dandelion would add. Wanders Far and Dandelion were also close, though they were different. No sooner would Wanders Far think a thought, and Dandelion would express it for him. It was as if they communicated telepathically. Bear Fat had wondered how it was possible that Dandelion could communicate such brilliant, seemingly original thoughts when Wanders Far was with him, but when Wanders Far was not at his side, Dandelion seemed to have difficulty finding anything important to say, though that never prevented him from talking. Nobody minded anyway, he was very friendly, and people enjoyed his light and breezy disposition.

Dandelion was 17-years-old. Two years earlier he had made the passage from boy to man. Yet he showed no signs of interest in Bear Fat's attempts to nudge him toward his future. He was happy as he was and was in no particular hurry to have his mother negotiate a marriage for him.

Summer at camp was not always full of leisure. There was plenty of work to do as well. By the time the summer was over, they had four bearskins, nine red-fox skins, six deerskins, a beaver, a martin, three skunks, and tons of dried meat, loads of dried blueberries, and another new birch bark canoe.

The birch trees that were so sought after were plentiful in the mountains. It was rare to find birch trees in the valleys where they made their homes, so the canoes they made in their village at Garoga Creek were constructed of elm bark, which was much heavier than canoes made of birch bark.

That summer, Wanders Far taught Gentle Breeze how to paddle a canoe and they made several trips, including paddling the entire perimeter of the figure-eight-shaped lake that was so calm it perfectly reflected the mountains that surrounded it. Wherever she went that summer, Gentle Breeze always seemed to position herself so that she was facing toward the majestic mountain.

As the family was packing to return home, Gentle Breeze realized that her necklace was missing. She hadn't thought of it all summer, and she had no idea how long it had been gone. The necklace was made up of a series of tiny charms carved by Red-Winged Blackbird. On special occasions, he would give her a new charm, mostly wood, but sometimes bone or shell, connected by twine. As she completed packing, she thought about her husband, how much she missed him, and she couldn't believe that he had been gone eleven years already. She shed a few tears as she worked, and it occurred to her that she was losing him just a little bit more now that the necklace was gone too. After a few minutes of sadness, she forced herself to think grateful thoughts about having the opportunity to spend the summer at the pond. Perhaps someone would find her necklace the following summer, she thought.

On the return trip toward their home to the south, Gentle Breeze managed the bow, while Wanders Far took the stern. Dandelion paddled the other small canoe by himself. The new canoe was a gift for Squash, Flint, and their family. They would be happy to receive it, and they wouldn't have believed it if they had seen it with their own eyes, to see Gentle Breeze paddling away in a canoe.

It was harvest time on the banks of Garoga Creek when they completed their return trip. For several months, Gentle Breeze, who was normally industrious in their village, and in her longhouse, was distracted, telling everyone about her summer. She confided to Bear Fat, the day after they returned, that over the course of that summer, she had been happier than she had ever been. Tears streaming down her face, she thanked her daughter for insisting that she join them at Copperas Pond.

Chapter Thirteen
Magic Crystal

The following summer, Bear Fat asked the boys and her husband to look everywhere they could to try and find Gentle Breeze's necklace. Bear Fat searched for it herself, looking under rocks, logs, and along the paths they customarily traveled. By the end of the summer, Bear Fat decided the necklace must be at the bottom of the pond, just beneath the ledge. The twine had probably broken when she jumped from the ledge into the water. Would the necklace sink? Would the necklace float? She hated to have to return home at the end of the summer without the keepsake, but it was not to be found.

After they returned to Garoga Creek, Wanders Far set out for a trip to Chipmunk's village. It had been a long time since anyone had seen his brother. Wanders Far's pack was filled with supplies, gifts for Chipmunk and his family. Even with a heavy pack, Wanders Far made good time, reaching the village late on the third day. His brother was happy to see him and Wanders Far was surprised to find that he had two nieces, rather than just one.

His timing was perfect, because the following day, Chipmunk and a group of men were headed southwest to mine salt near the south end of a long, narrow lake. Salt was a useful commodity. In addition to acting as a preservative, it was also very useful in curing hides and furs. Chipmunk suggested Wanders Far join them, and he could fill his backpack with salt for the return trip. They had to be careful to avoid enemies, who could also be making a trip in search of salt. Fortunately, it was late enough in the summer. The mining party was able to safely get to the cave of salt, fill their baskets and make a hasty retreat.

During the long, quiet march back from Cayuga Lake to the Oneida village, Wanders Far thought about Chipmunk. It was certainly nice to see him. He had been welcomed most politely. Yet somehow, Wanders Far felt like he was visiting a more distant relation than a brother. Maybe it was because he was so close to his brother Dandelion that he could read his youngest brother's mind. Perhaps it was the years between Chipmunk and Wanders Far, yet Wanders Far felt a brotherly connection with his warrior brother, Fisher, who was even older. He even felt a strong brotherly connection with Blue Arrow, from the tribe of his enemies and even Quahog, from the distant tribe near the ocean. Wanders Far concluded that he was grateful to have Chipmunk for a brother, even without any feeling of cosmic connectedness.

Wanders Far was making good time on the way back to Garoga Creek. He had one more long day of walking ahead of him. It was getting late in the afternoon and he decided to stop for the night at a wide, shallow river. The riverbanks were very flat, with lots of small pebbles and stones. He set his backpack down, and went to the river, where he finally found a good spot to submerge himself. After his swim, he returned to get his backpack. Wanders Far bent over to pick it up, and something caught his eye.

It wasn't a rock, exactly. Just lying among the stones was a large, clear, crystal gemstone, about half the size of his thumb. He put the gem in the palm of his hand, wrapped his fingers around it, and closed his eyes. He felt somehow connected to the stone. Did the stone have some kind of magical properties? He hesitated for a moment and then chuckled, admonishing himself for feeling connected to a rock, especially when he had recently felt disconnected from his blood brother just a few days earlier. He added the gemstone to his backpack and found a concealed spot under a tree near the river and settled in for the night.

Wanders Far awoke in the middle of the night after a strange dream. He had a vision of the rocky creek bed in which everything appeared to be the same gray color. The grass, the trees, the rocks, the water, all gray, but translucent. He realized that he could see beneath the surface, underground. There were millions of crystals lying about. In the dream they twinkled, shined, and sparkled, in contrast to the grayish color of everything that surrounded them. Wanders Far stayed awake just long enough to conclude he was meant to look for more of the gemstones the next day, then he returned to his slumber.

The next morning, he returned to the spot where he had found the gem. He spent the entire day hunched over, letting happenstance and his intuition guide him. He found similar gems of all different sizes, though mostly smaller than the first one he had found. In one day, he had amassed a sizable quantity of the curious rock. When he was done, Wanders Far returned to his campsite under the tree by the creek. Just as he had done with the first stone, he experimented with others, placing them in his hand, closing his eyes, and trying to determine their powers. The first stone seemed to have more power than the new ones, he thought.

When Wanders Far returned to his village late the next day, he brought the gemstones to their healer, the Bear Clan's medicine man. The healer held the bag of stones in his hands and closed his eyes as Wanders Far had done. He felt an instant spark of energy, like a tiny flash of lightening. He handed the bag back to Wanders Far. "Keep the first stone with you always," he advised. "Keep the rest in your home. Someday a wiser man than me will tell you what to do with them."

Wanders Far thanked the medicine man. He took the bag of stones home and tied it to his bunkbed frame. Squash tied the first stone for him, and attached it to a strong, fibrous cord for his neck. He smiled gratefully at his sister and put the necklace on. The smile dropped from his face instantly and he felt weak. He was unaccustomed to feeling weak. He took the necklace off and handed it back to Squash, and said, "The rock is upside-down."

Squash quickly flipped the stone and reattached it to the sinew. She held the talisman up to the light and felt its power. She glanced at Wanders Far. Sometimes she felt like she deeply understood her brother, and sometimes she felt like he was a complete mystery. In that moment, a fast but powerful feeling helped her understand a bit more. She handed the necklace back to him and said, "May it serve you well, Wanders Far."

Chapter Fourteen
Stealing Souvenirs from a Camp of Giants

O ne summer day around noon, a visitor announced himself from a distance, while the family was at Copperas Pond. The voice sounded familiar. Then, minutes later, Blue Arrow strolled into camp, greeting his old, adopted family as comfortably as if he had just seen them days earlier. Only it had been three years already since they had parted. Blue Arrow ignored the looks of astonishment on the faces of his old friends who hadn't expected to ever see him again.

"I have a surprise for you. You're going to love this. I left it just outside of your camp. Don't move a muscle. I'll be right back," Blue Arrow turned and raced out of sight for a minute. When he returned, he was carrying his backpack, and there was a blanket covering it.

Blue Arrow handed the basket to Bear Fat. "Go ahead, see what's under that blanket," he insisted.

Bear Fat tilted her head slightly and smiled. She was clearly amused, and not accustomed to many surprises. What she saw when she removed the blanket was shocking. She reached into the basket and pulled it out and held it to her chest. It licked her chin and yawned.

It was a small, black and fawn colored puppy, maybe 7-weeks-old. Dogs were not prevalent at that time. Some villages had a dog or two, but nobody could remember a dog having lived in the Bear Clan village. The dogs they had encountered in other villages were not cute, sweet, or fun. The puppy Blue Arrow brought was soft and fuzzy. It took Bear Fat's breath away. Big Canoe watched from a few feet away and wondered what they would do with such a useless present. Dandelion couldn't wait to get ahold of it. Wanders Far kept looking back and forth from the puppy to his mother, and occasionally to his old friend, Blue Arrow. "Can we name her Spirit?" Wanders Far asked.

Bear Fat replied, "I don't see why not," and Blue Arrow nodded.

Big Canoe and Dandelion looked at each other and shrugged. Big Canoe said, "I don't think that dog cares what you call it."

The puppy fell back to sleep on Bear Fat's chest, and everyone gathered around the fire pit. Blue Arrow told the story of how he and the other scouts had snuck into the camp of a very strange looking tribe of people and made off with a funny looking dog with a black muzzle, black cheeks, and a curly tail.

The dog ran off into the woods twice on the way back to Cave Eye. Blue Arrow and his companions followed. They tried to keep up the best they could. Then they heard barking, and a few seconds later, a big deer was running straight toward them. By habit, Blue Arrow grabbed his bow, notched an arrow, and dropped the deer. A couple of hours later they were passing along the edge of a large, wooded, marshy swamp. When they caught up to the barking dog she was harassing an angry, aggressive bull moose. She seemed to enjoy remaining just beyond its expansive rack. Moments later, Blue Arrow and two of his companions had sunk arrows into the moose. They were almost back to Cave Eye. The village would eat well, thanks to the stolen dog.

The dog was friendly. Everybody in the village loved her instantly. She was such a celebrity in the village that she never sought to leave to find her original owners. Two days after they arrived in the village, she gave birth to a large litter of puppies.

Curiously, Big Canoe asked Blue Arrow about the strange look-ing tribe of people. In no hurry, Blue Arrow told a proper story. Earlier that summer, he and his companions had become aware of a band of traveling strangers, heading north along the banks of the huge lake. They were a curious-looking party of about a dozen men. Blue Arrow described them as giant men, over six feet tall with thick, muscular arms and legs, like tree trunks. They had long, wavy hair flowing from their heads and faces, and wore hats with horns. Some had white hair, some had yellow hair, and several had orange hair. They spoke an unknown language, and often barked and grunted at each other. They made so much noise, it was easy to follow them. Blue Arrow and his party had seen enough and were just about ready to return home when the men went down to the lake, leaving their camp unattended, and leaving the dog tied to a tree. It was easy to make off with the dog and many other unusual souvenirs from their camp. Blue Arrow assured Big Canoe that by the time the men re-turned from the lake, he and his friends were long gone.

Wanders Far asked about the lake. Blue Arrow told them about a lake so huge it took days to paddle from top to bottom, and hours to paddle across. Blue Arrow offered to take Wanders Far to see it. Dandelion joked, "If you take him to see it, he'll want to see the whole thing."

In case Dandelion thought he might remain at Copperas Pond, Big Canoe said, "Good thing we've finished our bear hunting here for the summer, because I know you will want to join them, Dandelion. I know you'll want to see the whole thing too, and they can make great use of your paddling skills." Dandelion understood that his father was sending him to protect Wanders Far from hordes of strange, long-haired giants on the lake.

The next morning, Wanders Far and Dandelion followed Blue Arrow out of camp, carrying their newest canoe, completed just days earlier. It was a sizable canoe, with plenty of room for all three of them. They headed due east, and two days later, they arrived at a large bay. They dropped the canoe in the lake and paddled due north. It was a clear and sunny day. There was no wind, and the lake was unusually still. The three friends began a week-long adventure. They explored the shores and islands of the great lake, with no other purpose or sense of urgency.

The explorers returned ten days later. They were just in time. Big Canoe and Bear Fat were ready to make the long, return trip back to Garoga Creek. The puppy had almost doubled in size. Wanders Far and Dandelion were surprised to see that Spirit followed Big Canoe everywhere he went. Bear Fat told them that Big Canoe had a new love in his life. Big Canoe grinned, and said, "I'm sure I'll have to share her when we get home."

The next morning the friends parted, with hopes they would see each other again soon. Blue Arrow asked them to tell everyone he missed them, especially Gentle Breeze. Bear Fat, Big Canoe, Dandelion, Wanders Far, and tiny Spirit began the long journey to Garoga Creek.

Their return home usually caused a commotion, as Bear Fat and her family generously shared the abundance of their summer hunting and gathering. Big Canoe was right to predict that Spirit would become the center of attention for the village. Overnight, Spirit became the village mascot. She didn't mind all of the attention, but always returned to Big Canoe's side.

Gentle Breeze loved to run her fingers through the puppy's fuzzy fur. From the moment she heard that the puppy's name was Spirit, she assumed that she could communicate with Red-Winged Blackbird, just by talking to the dog. She knew that everyone was laughing at her, but she didn't care. It made her happy, and Spirit seemed to like it also. One day, Wanders Far whispered to his grandmother, "I think you are right. Grandfather hears you when you talk to that puppy, and it makes Grandfather's spirit happy. Don't listen to everybody else. I think you should just go right on ahead and talk to Grandfather. Maybe that's why the puppy was sent to us."

As summer ended, Bear Fat's happy family grew a little larger. In the middle of the annual corn harvest, Squash gave birth to a baby girl. Bear Fat had attended many births in her years. Moments after the baby was born, Bear Fat wrapped her newest granddaughter in a warm fur blanket and proclaimed proudly, "This is the most beautiful baby I have ever seen." She looked at Squash and they shared a warm smile. Mother and baby both took a well-deserved nap.

Chapter Fifteen
A Malevolent Presence

The following year Bear Fat, Big Canoe, Dandelion, and Wanders Far returned to Garoga Creek from Copperas Pond just after the corn harvest. Wanders Far didn't even stop by his own compartment and went directly to see his niece, who had been named Somersault while they were away. He couldn't wait to see how much she had grown.

First, he hugged Squash, and then he picked up the little girl who had been playing with some twigs and stones by the hearth. He gave her a hug, pecked her cheek with dozens of kisses, and then sat down by the fire with her.

Squash watched her brother and her daughter while she wove a blanket. What was it about her daughter, she wondered? It wasn't just her baby brother that was drawn to that child. Squash felt a glimmer within her soul, stopped her weaving briefly, clasped her hands together on her chest, and rested her chin on her knuckles. My baby girl has a grand purpose, she thought.

The next day Quahog, the Narraganset trader, returned. Since his first visit seven years earlier, he had included the Garoga Creek village on his regular annual route. People enjoyed his visits and looked forward to trading with him. When he completed his bartering, Quahog made a deal to hire Dandelion and Wanders Far to escort him westward to fill more baskets with trade goods. Quahog also attempted to make a deal with Wanders Far for the enormous thumb-shaped quartz crystal on his chest. Wanders Far told him not to worry. He added, "Perhaps you can find your own along the way." They were headed that direction anyhow.

The next morning, Wanders Far untied the bag of crystals from his bunk. He hadn't given them much thought since tying them there two years earlier. Before they set out on the trail, Wanders Far asked Squash's husband if he could work with the crystals. Flint was an expert at crafting stone into implements, such as knives, axes, and arrowheads. Flint tried to get an idea what he should turn them into, but Wanders Far offered him no guidance, except to say, "Hold one in the palm of your hands, and close your eyes. It will come to you."

A couple weeks later, the travelers found themselves in a small village on a high bluff overlooking a lake so big they couldn't see all the way across it. They referred to the lake as the Shining Waters. Quahog had spent several hours, negotiating trades with the people there. All morning, a woman had been trying to trade the largest, and best-crafted corn dolls they had ever seen, complete with clothing and jewelry. "What would I do with these?" Quahog asked honestly.

"I might be interested in one of those," Wanders Far shrugged. He had learned from Quahog that it was important to seem some-what indifferent when making a barter. He made a show of trying to differentiate between the three large dolls the woman had with her. She dragged him back to her longhouse. He tried to protest, but without success. When he walked through the door he thought, *If I am having trouble choosing between three dolls, how would choosing among dozens of them make things easier!* Until he saw the perfect doll. It looked exactly like his favorite niece, complete with dimples. Beyond the watchful eye of Quahog, Wanders Far completed a most generous trade. The Cayuga woman was deliriously happy. Most of the people made their own dolls. She rarely got more than smiles from grateful children for her handiwork.

Quahog, Dandelion, and Wanders Far spent the rest of the day wandering along the shore of the lake. Their hosts guided them along the trail to elevated bluffs above the lake. For a long time, they stood at the edge of a cliff, three hundred feet above the surface of the lake, looking out over the glistening, Shining Waters. Immediately over the edge of the cliff there were giant rock formations, mud-colored spires, tortuously sculpted by the elements throughout the ages.

When the others had tired of standing at the precipice, they followed the trail which crossed the bluff then led down the hill to the shore. After a while, Wanders Far was alone. He stood at the edge of the precipice and stretched his arms as wide as he possibly could.

A bald eagle soared into view, looking for a meal, scampering along the exposed terrain. Wanders Far thought the eagle had quite an advantage.

He concentrated and visualized himself seeing the view from the eagle's perspective. Remarkably, he felt the sensation of his soul leaving his body. Then he felt the spirit of the bird. There was a feeling of hunger, and a need to feed. Wanders Far felt a malevolent presence. The bird was an inhospitable host for the boy and was eager to return to the work of finding a meal.

Briefly, the eagle tolerated the boy's pointless flight. He spread his wings wide and effortlessly glided across the top of the prominent formations, then tilted effortlessly to the left and flew out over the water. Wanders Far saw himself standing on the edge of the far away cliff through the eagle's eyes way out over the open water. Then the eagle tilted again, turning back toward the dunes.

The eagle's eye caught sight of a medium sized jackrabbit near the bottom of a hill, slightly to the west of the cliffs, a very short distance from the pebble beach where Wanders Far's hosts and companions stood, feet in the water. Wanders Far got a sense that the bird had forgotten that it was carrying him along with it. The bird flew faster, and faster, directly toward the rabbit. Wanders Far felt like the bird would smash itself onto the ground, rendered lifeless by the contact. Yet the boy felt the excitement of the speed, feeling the air pass over the wings of the bird, and the sense of conquest. He felt the need to snatch the rabbit from the ground with the bird's sharp yellow toes. Moments later, Wanders Far felt the rush of danger that came with approaching the ground and grabbing the rabbit. The possibility of a violent impact and the proximity of a fixed surface was exciting. Fortunately, the eagle expertly avoided a collision without thought or plan, but rather with a skill perfected by years of experience.

As the bird rose again into the air, he seemed to remember that he was carrying an extra spirit, which he no longer was interested in entertaining. The bird gained elevation, and as the eagle flew over the body of Wanders Far, the eagle defecated. Wanders Far felt his spirit return to his own body just in time to experience the sensation of a glob of wet bird excrement land on the back of his neck.

The eagle landed twenty-five feet from Wanders Far. With a few quick movements, beak and talons ripped the rabbit's body to shreds. Wanders Far watched as the eagle had his meal. Wanders Far felt the bird's spirit gloating and taunting the boy, as if it was intentionally depriving Wanders Far of the experience of enjoying the meal. Nonetheless, Wanders Far concentrated on sending a message of gratitude back to the bird, appreciation for the gift of flight and the chance to experience the scenery from a different perspective.

Moments later, the eagle took off from the cliffs and Wanders Far watched until he disappeared into the distance. When he was gone, Wanders Far followed the path westward, down the hill, and then turned to walk along the pebble beach where he caught up with the others.

"Did you see that magnificent eagle?" Dandelion shouted as Wanders Far approached.

Wanders Far nodded, put a slight, mock frown on his face, stretched his arms as he had on the bluff, and slowly spun around, showing his brother the mess he carried on his back.

Dandelion hooted and hollered, jumped up and down, and shouted, "Is that what I think it is?" Dandelion got so excited, it was as if he were envious that his brother had been singled out to receive a great gift. "I never heard of anybody getting crapped on by an eagle."

Wanders Far shook his head in disbelief. Normally his brother was so relaxed and easy going, nothing much seemed to get him going. Of all the things they experienced together through the years, Wanders Far thought, it took eagle poop for him to find a way to entertain his brother.

Dandelion made sure every member of their host party got a good look before he let his brother wash himself off in the lake. "Have you had enough yet?" Wanders Far finally asked his brother. Then he turned toward the Shining Waters and waded out until the water was deep enough to swim in.

As he bathed, Wanders Far reflected on being carried by the eagle. He had never felt his spirit in the body of an animal before. The only human body Wanders Far could recall sending his spirit into was his brother, Dandelion. Wanders Far chuckled at the thought that the bird knew he was there, but his brother never did. It was a one-way spiritual connection. Wanders Far could read his brother's thoughts as his brother conjured them and Wanders Far could place his own thoughts in his brother's mind whenever he wished. On his way back from the water, Wanders Far admonished himself for thinking the eagle was smarter than his brother. The fact was, Wanders Far adored and idolized his carefree sibling.

The next morning, they headed for home. The three large

backpacks they carried were filled to overflowing. The villagers saw them off at dawn. The woman who sold Wanders Far the doll was there. Before they disappeared over the hillside, Wanders Far turned around, faced the villagers and held the two-foot tall doll up in his outstretched arms. The people cheered and Wanders Far bowed. He hoped that he had helped increase the dollmaker's notoriety.

The doll definitely caught people's attention when Wanders Far carried it through the palisade walls of his home village. Nobody had ever seen anything like it. People were thinking, "Who spends that much time and effort, and devotes that much valuable material to construct a child's plaything?" Nevertheless, a large group of curious children followed Wanders Far through the village to his longhouse. Somersault stood close to her mother's side when she saw Wanders Far and the doll, apprehensive. Wanders Far stood the doll a comfortable distance from Somersault and said, "She's all yours!"

Other girls in the village had dolls. Simple dolls constructed from dried, folded-over corn leaves, no taller than a cob of corn. Somersault quickly warmed to the idea of such a plaything. She gave the doll a quick hug, then raised her tiny arms in the air toward Wanders Far, indicating that she would like to be lifted up to give him a hug too.

Before dawn, they were back on the trail again. For a few days they traveled by canoe, then they hiked five days before arriving in Quahog's village.

Quahog arrived to a hero's welcome. It had become an annual tradition. It was as if he were bringing everyone luxurious gifts. In reality, it was his people's hard work that paid for the trades. Dandelion stood on one side of Quahog and Wanders Far stood on the other side. One by one, Quahog introduced everyone to his traveling companions, and every resident of the village received something from the three backpacks he brought.

Then they feasted on clams and corn. Dandelion and Wanders Far had never tasted the clams before.

The following day Quahog led them to the ocean, where they played in the waves like children, and giggled like babies at the miracle of the sand, and the waves. After a couple of hours of enjoying the beach, Wanders Far filled his backpack with seaweed and collected as many seashells as he could. He topped his heavy load off with a perfectly proportioned dried starfish he found on the beach, another gift for Somersault.

When they returned to Garoga Falls, Flint gave Wanders Far the magic crystals. He and Squash had discussed it, and they had worked together to make each crystal into a necklace, and they had crafted a small box to contain each one. They thought it would be a good idea for the boxes and necklaces to be gifts for the future.

Wanders Far thanked Flint and Squash and resolved to place the boxes of necklaces under rocks whenever he had the chance.

Chapter Sixteen
Great Roaring Waterfalls

B ear Fat and Big Canoe took advantage of their son's wander-lust, sending countless messages to their extended families in distant villages. Bear Fat figured if she sent him with a message and a purpose, however mundane, at least she'd know approximately where he was going, and perhaps when he might return.

From time to time, he would travel with the professional run-ners, mostly men in their twenties, who would carry official mes-sages to other villages and tribes, near and far. Each time, Bear Fat received the news that Wanders Far had been no trouble, kept up with the pace, and did not hold back the forward progress of the men who travel great distances. Wanders Far never complained even when an urgent matter would require a grueling pace, or when im-mediate turn-around was necessary. After years of training, his legs never seemed to tire. Whenever he was awake, his legs were moving.

Summer was over, and it was early autumn. Wanders Far hap-pened to be passing through the Turtle Clan village, a few miles to the southwest of his own village. Chief Warm Welcome asked him to carry an official message to all the neighboring villages and friendly tribes that the Turtle Clan was hosting a tournament. The event would be held in three weeks. Wanders Far had to get the word out fast. He had many miles to travel, and many villages to inform.

Chief Warm Welcome was not disappointed. The tournament brought lots of visitors, and the population of his village quadrupled in size for a couple of days. Many folks came to participate in the competition, and plenty more came to watch. Families had the chance to connect with distant family members, and old friends were reunited. It was also an occasion for trading goods. Many people arrived with a giant basket strapped to their back, full of one thing, and then returned home after the tournament with a basket full of something else. Another benefit of hosting such a tournament was the chance that the unmarried maidens of the village would have a chance to catch the eyes of eligible young bachelors, or perhaps more importantly the eyes of mothers who were responsible for arranging and negotiating marriages.

Around the campfire, the night before the first game, a large group of young men boasted loudly about their athletic abilities. Someone suggested an endurance challenge. An epic race, all the way to the land of the Great Roaring Waterfalls, and then back again, for a total distance of five-hundred miles. The race would take them through the territory of several friendly tribes, and many villages of each tribe at that, but also through enemy lands nearest the Waterfalls. About a dozen men committed to the event, each more boastful than the previous. Finally, Wanders Far, in a matter-of-fact voice, proclaimed that he would beat them all. The others laughed. He was by far the youngest in the crowd, and small compared to other 14-year-olds. It was clear that they didn't see him as a threat. Plans were finalized for a race to begin ten days later.

A wandering sachem known to all the tribes as He Who Follows the Stars agreed to set out in the morning for the Great Roaring Waterfalls. When he was a younger man, he had been a runner, and as a man of 60 he still traveled great distances. Through the years, he also became a seer, a healer, and a craftsman, creating treasured talismans to bring good luck and blessings from the Great Spirit to those who were lucky enough to receive a small carved figure, painted rock, or necklace from Follows Stars. The next morning, as the sachem set out for the checkpoint at the Waterfalls, the lacrosse tournament got underway.

Wanders Far and his older brother Dandelion were on one of three teams representing the Bear Clan village. Dandelion was an expert lacrosse player. He was the star player on a team full of strong players. Wanders Far was the weakest player on their team. After a couple of days of competition, their team had reached the semifinals. In a close game, they were eliminated, and thus became spectators for the final game.

The entire village, residents, and visitors celebrated each evening. After the first day of games, Dandelion met a sad girl his age. She was mourning the loss of her husband who had been killed in a raid on an Algonquin hunting party at the beginning of the summer. They were newlyweds, very much in love, and he was a wonderful husband. Sadly, he wasn't a very good warrior, and he was the only member of their village who had been lost to their enemies in the past several years. Dandelion had taken a liking to her and did his best to cheer her up, lifting her spirits with his easygoing nature, funny stories, and friendly demeanor. By the time the tournament concluded, their affections drove them into a passion that engulfed them and Wanders Far was sent home to bring the family. Bear Fat quickly arranged and negotiated a marriage for her third son. She had been trying to convince Dandelion for a couple of years that it was time to find a wife. He was 21-years-old, after all.

Several more racers were added to the roster in the final days leading up to the start of the race. Whoever won the race would become wealthy. Each contestant brought a stack of furs considered equal to the value of one bearskin. The entry fees were held by Warm Welcome in trust for the eventual winner of the race. The race would begin the morning after the final lacrosse game, an hour after sunrise.

Wanders Far, who had hadn't whined about anything since he was a toddler, hobbled to the starting line, lower lip extended into a petulant pout, and whimpered quietly as if he were a child in pain. Inside he was chuckling, certain that he would be passing many of these older, stronger racers in the days to come. All the other contestants were men, having completed their rites of passage.

An hour after the sun came up on the first day, Warm Welcome counted down from ten, then raised his arms as high in the air as he could. The contestants sprinted out of camp, hastily making their way onto the path as if the race was a sprint. Wanders Far limped out of camp, favoring what looked to be a sore ankle. Those who didn't know Wanders Far thought he would be back within an hour. He turned toward his family, found his mother's eyes, and smiled, ever so slightly. Bear Fat was there to cheer on her son, and smiled, shaking her head. She couldn't imagine what had possessed him to pretend an injury. Didn't he have enough of a challenge to cover five-hundred miles faster than sixteen full-grown men? She was glad that she wasn't competing in such a race.

After the first hour, Wanders Far lost sight of the next slowest racer. All day long, he walked at his usual brisk pace, a pace he knew he could maintain endlessly, without ever tiring.

For several months, Wanders Far had been experiencing glimpses of a vision. The visions came to him in tiny flickers. Every flicker of a vision was of the same person. Of a man. A man unlike Wanders Far had ever seen. His skin was pale, almost white. Instead of black hair, he had long, flowing, light brown hair, plentiful on his face as well as flowing from the top of his head. Wanders Far felt like he was looking at that man through the icy surface of a frozen pond. That first day on the long trail, the flickers lengthened to the point where Wanders Far could make out scenes of several seconds in duration.

Over and over, he saw the man in tattered, dusty white robes, standing on the slight incline of a hill, talking to a crowd of several dozen people who stared at him adoringly. The other aspect of the vision that struck Wanders Far was that beyond the strange color of his skin, the man seemed to glow, radiating light as if he had swallowed the moon, and he had a warm, happy, serene look on his face. He seemed to be saying to the crowd, "Everything will be alright." He seemed to be saying the same thing to Wanders Far, as well.

Ten hours later, Wanders Far saw five other racers ahead of him. They were lounging about on the limbs of an old tree, gorging themselves on apples. Wanders Far picked up one apple and continued on. An hour later, he passed another group of racers who had stopped to rest. There were still several hours of daylight. Wanders Far passed them as well. Two hours later, Wanders Far approached an encampment. The rest of the racers had settled in for the night, hours earlier, after a day of running. Wanders Far greeted them kindly, and, limping again, kept on going. Perhaps they didn't know there was a village just an hour away. Wanders Far knew he would be there just after sunset. When he arrived in the village, he was given a warm bowl of venison and offered a comfortable bunk for the night. Wanders Far was asleep instantly, and back on the trail an hour before dawn.

A couple of hours after Wanders Far began his second day, a large group of racers jogged past Wanders Far, chuckling, and taunting him with insults. It was all in good fun. Wanders Far shrugged, as if to suggest that he never should have tried to best them in the first place. By noon, the rest of the racers had passed him as well. He waved graciously as they passed him, as if to wish them well, and congratulate them on their progress.

Several times that second day, Wanders Far experienced the visions he had on the first day, and also other small scenes of the same man in different situations. The man was in a village instead of on a hillside, and the village was full of small longhouses, square instead of rectangular. They looked like they were made of clay. The people who lived in that village seemed miserable and unhappy, with faces full of worry. Then the man in the dream would put his hand on their shoulders, or kiss their foreheads, and suddenly those people seemed to have their hearts healed. It looked like he was sharing his power with them and yet he never seemed to run out of power. Maybe he was a healer, or a man who carried the Great Spirit's heart. Instead of seeing the same vision over and over, Wanders Far saw the same story repeated, but with different people being comforted.

By the end of the day, Wanders Far passed all the racers and kept on going. He spent the night in an abandoned hut by a small stream, which he had correctly predicted would be unoccupied. Wanders Far knew that hut well and used it on previous trips.

The next two days continued on much the same way as the first two had. Some of the fastest racers were starting to wonder how Wanders Far managed to continue along as far as he had, catching up every day, and with an injured ankle, no less. The lead pack determined to move even quicker, and leave Wanders Far way behind, and for that matter, the rest of the lagging racers as well. It was time to whittle the herd down to a few men who had an honest chance of winning. Then that group could determine the winner on the final day in an epic, grueling battle.

The lead group jogged most of the fifth day, pushing themselves almost to the limits of their endurance. They made several lengthy stops to catch their breath. Wanders Far, however, took no breaks, and didn't change his pace in the slightest. The wiry muscles in his spindly legs were as fresh as they had been on the first day. It was well after dark when Wanders Far caught up with the lead racers, who were all fast asleep under a large maple tree. He thought the moon provided enough light to continue on. The terrain was flat, the path was impossible to mistake, and by midnight, he happened to wander upon a lean-to, complete with an abandoned elkskin, which provided a relaxing, quick night's sleep.

Again, on the sixth day, Wanders Far got an early start. The lead racers were astonished when they trotted past him at noon. Instead of taunting, the lead man, Slingshot, asked Wanders Far how on earth he had managed to pass them. He asked, "Are you a real boy, or a spirit?"

Wanders Far shrugged in his typical fashion. "You were all sleeping like a bunch of babies when I passed your camp last night. Good thing there are no Algonquins on the trail," he added. Wanders Far couldn't help but notice that a few of his opponents' faces appeared worried at the mention of their enemies. He wondered if it was possible that they hadn't thought of that.

A couple of hours later, Wanders Far caught up with them again. They had finally reached the thunderous, raging waterfalls. Some were stretched out along the river, basking in the sun, and others were swimming in the swift river. They were so relaxed, they hadn't even noticed that Wanders Far had caught up. He continued on to find the checkpoint.

Follows Stars had constructed a small, temporary encampment right on the bank of the wide river, just above the waterfall. He had been there several days, and had become quite comfortable, passing time by whittling warriors, scouts, and hunters four inches tall. He had carved one runner. He smiled when he saw Wanders Far approach his camp. He knew that Wanders Far would get there first. Follows Stars had visualized Wanders Far's arrival, and his smile broadened as the boy got closer.

Follows Stars gave Wanders Far a small rock with a turtle painted on the top and one hashmark painted on the bottom. They talked for a couple minutes and the seer congratulated the boy. Then he asked Wanders Far if he had encountered any difficulty finding the checkpoint.

Wanders Far told him, "No, I just imagined where you would be, and there you were!" The seer gave him a bowl of buffalo meat with a thick gravy. Then the seer handed him some cornbread with sunflower seeds and dried blueberries baked into it. It was a heavy meal. Wanders Far ate a few bites and thanked him, passing the bowl back. Buffalo was a rare treat, since most of their villages were just outside of the Buffalo's normal range.

Follows Stars could have predicted the boy would only eat a little. He closed his eyes and reached for Wanders Far's hands. After a silent minute, the seer completed his reading. Follows Stars thought, *This is the boy I always knew would come.* The old man opened his eyes. Wanders Far had been gazing at the lids of the eyes of the old seer. Wanders Far felt a strong energy pass through his torso, not from the hands of the seer, but rather through the very air. It was a happy, comforting feeling of connectedness, not just to the current time and place, the man standing in front of him and the task at hand, but to humanity throughout the ages past, and those yet to come. The seer asked the boy, "Did you see anything?"

Wanders Far said, "No, I felt it. You have a glorious spirit."

Follows Stars whispered, "That was exactly what I was going to say to you!" A couple of silent moments passed, and the seer released the boy's hands. "I want you to have this," he said, giving Wanders Far the runner he had carved. It looked just like the boy, only a year or two older.

The whole visit lasted ten minutes. After he said goodbye to the seer, Wanders Far stood facing the Great Roaring Waterfalls. For ninety seconds, he soaked it in. Wanders Far felt that he had stayed too long as it was. He was only halfway finished. He took a quick drink of water and was back on the trail, again passing the men who had stopped to rest at the river, without them even knowing he had been there. Wanders Far wondered what they would think when they discovered that rock number 1 had already been taken. He chuckled at the thought, and walked well past dark, again reaching the abandoned lean-to that he had slept in the night before, only that night it wasn't abandoned. It was full of sleeping racers. Wanders Far quietly found an unoccupied corner and quickly fell asleep.

All of the racers were up early on the seventh morning. A good night's sleep had done them all a lot of good, and they were in high spirits, expecting to reach the Great Roaring Waterfalls later that day. They noticed that Wanders Far had caught up to them and congratulated him on his persistence. They hadn't expected him to make it that far, figuring he would have turned around for home way before that point. When everyone was ready to continue, they all started down the path toward the checkpoint. Wanders Far headed the opposite way.

"Giving up this close to the checkpoint," one of the younger men chided. Wanders Far just shrugged, hung his head, and gave a sad, weak, defeated wave in parting.

That morning, he heard them before he saw them. The fast seven were still traveling together. After learning from the old man at the checkpoint that Wanders Far beat them to the mid-point, they had found some respect for the kid. None of them expected that he would win, but when they caught up with him they slowed from their jog to a walk, and congratulated him for hanging in there, doing so well, and wished him well on the back half of the race. He had earned their respect. The fast seven took off at a run, and the last of the seven told Wanders Far that he'd see him back at the Turtle Clan village. Then Wanders Far was left alone, the eighth racer in a field of seventeen.

The lead group put in a solid day. Instead of breaking early, they pushed themselves right up to dusk, then sacked out on the sandy banks of a babbling brook. Wanders Far didn't catch up with them that day but spent the night in a nest of leaves a quarter of a mile behind them, and got a nourishing night's sleep. The lead racers weren't so lucky. It got cold that night, and the temperatures dropped significantly. Fall was fast approaching. They woke up before dawn, not refreshed at all, and quickly put their feet back on the trail, moving as slowly as they possibly could while still being able to call it a run.

It didn't warm up much on the eighth day, and to make matters worse, it started to rain around noon—just a chilly drizzle at first—then a constant, steady rain with no wind. That was followed by driving rains with blustery winds, which forced the rain to fall sideways, weaponizing each tiny rain drop. The drops stung. Wanders Far clenched his teeth, and thought, *This is where I win!* He had endured similar tortuous storms during past journeys. He neither quickened nor slackened his pace, but merely fortified his reserve of determination with the belief that scrawny or not, he was trained to deal with such adversity. He dared Mother Nature to do her worst. That she did.

The lead racers found a bit of natural shelter and huddled up within it, sharing each other's warmth as best they could. It was a miserable night. It was raining so hard, they didn't hear Wanders Far pass them on the trail three hours before dark, not that any of the racers saw the sun go over the western horizon that night. The trail at that point was well worn and Wanders Far knew his feet could follow the trail even if he couldn't see where it was headed. The land was flat. Fortunately, the rain stopped just before dark. Wanders Far kept walking. Gradually the clouds lifted. A warm front rode in on the backside of the storm, and it got warmer as the evening went on. An hour later the sky was cloudless, and the moon, almost full, shone brightly. Wanders Far thought to stop but didn't feel tired. He felt jubilant. He outlasted the storm and was putting himself farther ahead of the competition. There would be no comforting pile of leaves that night, but around midnight, an opportunity at the side of the trail presented itself, a natural depression in a bank, a foot and a half in elevation above the trail, and miraculously it was bone dry. It was just the right size for a boy like him.

The ninth day was an ordinary day but Wanders Far's spirits remained high. He began to feel like he was getting closer to the finish line. Occasionally, adrenaline would surge through his body as he visualized himself winning the race. He maintained his constant pace and as he walked through the day, he asked himself why he cared if he won anyhow. After pondering that question all day long, he found no answer. Part of the reason he never excelled at lacrosse was that he really never cared if he won or lost. Maybe it just wasn't his thing. It wasn't for the glory; Wanders Far never sought to be the center of attention, but rather shied away from it. Perhaps it was just the respect of other runners that motivated him. Whatever the reason, something was driving him forward, and what others his age could never accomplish, never even felt like a chore for him. Wanders Far relished the journey.

The nearer he got to the finish line, the more familiar the surroundings. He felt he could almost walk those trails in his sleep. He expected the other racers to run throughout the final night, pushing hard to beat one another. He was sure they thought he had been left behind during the rainstorm. While he remained convinced that he was way ahead, he didn't want to leave anything to chance. It was day ten. It should take twelve-and-a-half days to complete the race. He thought he was well ahead of the pace, having shortened the nights from both ends. If he walked throughout the tenth night, perhaps he could arrive in the Turtle Clan village around midnight on the eleventh day.

As the sun came up on day number eleven, Wanders Far finished the dried, jerked meat and berries in the small pouch tied to his waistband. He drank deeply from the river that would come to be named after the people of his tribe. The cold water was so brisk and refreshing, he decided to jump into the water. After slapping his face with cupped handfuls of river water, he returned to the trail. He traveled at the same pace, but he felt more awake after his quick dunk in the cold water. The adrenaline rush returned again and again as the day progressed. It was familiar territory and he walked it in a trance, almost as if he had been sleepwalking.

As the sun set behind him, he came upon a small bluff with a good view of the trail behind him. He turned and looked carefully. He could see a great distance, and there was no sign of the other racers. He maintained his pace. The camp drew nearer.

Four hours after dark, he was sure that everyone in the village was asleep. They wouldn't expect any of the racers to arrive that night.

Wanders Far quietly slipped into the village. He hated to awaken the chief with his inconvenient arrival, but Warm Welcome instructed the racers to do so if they arrived while he was sleeping. He was fortunate to find the chief awake, having just put wood on his fire. Instead of returning to bed, the chief stood outside to talk with Wanders Far. The chief congratulated him earnestly, draping his arm over the boy's back and clenching his shoulder on the other side. In his other hand, Warm Welcome had another rock with his own thumbprint on one side and one hashmark on the other side. He placed the rock on the palm of Wanders Far's right hand and told him to get a good night sleep.

The chief helped Wanders Far carry the pile of prize skins to the entrance of the village and instructed Wanders Far to stack them up in a mound and then make himself cozy and comfortable in them. It was a beautiful night to sleep out under the stars. He was asleep seconds after he jumped onto the stack of furs. The chief looked at him for a few minutes and shook his head from side to side, in wondrous amazement that one so small could accomplish such a feat. He knew that the boy was 14-years-old, practically a man, but lying there, lost in the furs, with just his head poking out, he looked more like 10, or even 9-years-old. On the way back to his own furs, a vision of Wanders Far's future flashed through the chief's consciousness. He felt it but he couldn't describe the vision. Perhaps it would come to him again. Perhaps Follows Stars could explain what it meant.

Indeed, the fast seven did endeavor to walk through the final night. A couple of hours past dark, one of the seven tripped over an exposed root, and twisted his ankle. He had been exhausted anyhow and used the excuse to pause for the night. His brother-in-law decided to stay with him.

In the middle of the night, three of the final five picked up the pace, jogging, running in single file. The other two didn't have any run left in them.

The first light appeared as a smudge on the horizon, and Slingshot suddenly began to run faster. It was time to leave the others behind. The other two accelerated as well. For the next hour they traded positions, taking turns leading, and gradually the shortest of the three, a 20-year-old man called War Paint, pulled into the lead. The third man was known as He Who Must Win, and his displeasure at being in third place showed on his face.

It was an hour after dawn. Wanders Far was still asleep on his mound of furs. The village had been told of the approaching runners, and they quietly spilled outside of the opening between the palisade walls and formed a long line on each side of the path, to welcome the runners in.

The village was within sight. Slingshot fell to third, as He Who Must Win found the competitive energy needed to dart past him, then also past War Paint. Each man put in the maximum energy they could muster after a dozen days and five-hundred miles of racing. With a final burst of energy in the final three-hundred yards, Slingshot sped past his friends, crossing the threshold before them. He was still running at top speed when he saw the stack of furs right in front of him, too late to stop. Arms and legs flailing, in an attempt to slow down, Slingshot landed on top of the pile, and crashed into Wanders Far who was just waking up, bewildered, having slept later than he could ever remember sleeping before.

Warm Welcome stood a few feet away, laughing heartily at the sight, which unfolded just as he had hoped it would. Slingshot was surprised at the ridiculousness of the situation, and overcome with raucous laughter, partly due to lack of sleep and partly due to physical exertion. He was glad the race was over. Then all of a sudden it occurred to him. The sleeping boy in the pile of prize furs at the entrance to the village meant that the boy had won the race. Slingshot was a good-natured competitor, and heartily congratulated the boy, telling Wanders Far that he was the better man, and that he considered him a brother. He Who Must Win wasn't as good a sport. It was a good thing for Wanders Far that Slingshot also beat He Who Must Win across the finish line, because it was clear that He Who Must Win could easily become He Who Holds a Grudge. Wanders Far thought of the other competitors. It occurred to him that it must be hard to be a good sport when you spend twelve days in pursuit of victory, and it must be hard when you are a man to be beaten by a boy.

Warm Welcome escorted the three racers to comfortable bunks in the village so that they could get some well-deserved rest, then returned to the village gates. Wanders Far was awake for the day and answering questions, telling everyone the story of the race. Warm Welcome thought, *He may look like a boy, but that one is a man now.*

Chapter Seventeen
He Who Follows the Stars

The winter that followed was hard on the village at Garoga Creek. It was longer, colder, and snowier than usual. Due to a great harvest the year before, there was still plenty of corn, beans, and squash, but other provisions had run low by the time spring came along.

During the course of the fall, winter, and spring, Wanders Far experienced a long overdue growth spurt. In a few short months, he left behind the scrawny, undersized boy who managed to beat the men on the race to the Great Roaring Waterfalls, to become a slender young man of average height. He was still much shorter than his father, who was the tallest man in the village. In addition to being taller than he had been a year earlier, Wanders Far's shoulders were broader. On his upper body, a modest measure of strength had begun to manifest, with a little musculature developing in his arms and on his chest, and his legs appeared far less spindly. His hips remained slim, with no fat on his stomach, and his waist was still narrow.

Merely one week after the ice melted from the surface of the lakes and ponds, the family ventured out on the trail. Bear Fat thought about how much effort it took when she had a larger family to tend. It didn't take long to prepare for the trip anymore.

Follows Stars, the wandering seer, arrived in the Bear Clan

village near the end of winter. The previous year, before the seer left for the Great Roaring Waterfalls to set up a checkpoint, Big Canoe had asked him if he would join their family for their summer trip to the mountains. He wanted the seer to guide Wanders Far's passage into manhood.

The trip started with a four-day hike from their home on Garoga Creek to Moose River. Bear Fat had been busy tending to the affairs of the families in her longhouse, as well as in her village. Until they started that journey, she hadn't spent much time thinking about the change in their family dynamics.

Bear Fat thought that Big Canoe would have a difficult summer. He had lost his protégé, business partner, and best friend. If he had to be honest, Dandelion was his favorite child. Bear Fat reflected that her husband was a good man and a good father to all of their children, but it was impossible to hide the fact that Dandelion and Big Canoe shared a unique bond that others couldn't intrude upon.

Following Dandelion's marriage the previous fall, Bear Fat turned her thoughts and attention to Wanders Far. He had turned 15-years-old. Most men married between the ages of 18 and 20. Dandelion took longer. Her first and second sons had married sooner. Bear Fat wasn't in a particular hurry to marry off her boys and move them out of her village, especially her last boy, but she felt a solemn responsibility to help them find and develop their talents, discover their futures, and realize their maximum potential.

The day after Dandelion moved out, Wanders Far noticed the watchful eye of his mother. He wondered if she always watched over him in that manner, and he merely had not noticed before.

Bear Fat wondered whether anyone could tell that Wanders Far was, to her, the most precious among her children. As a leader, she worked hard to treat people consistently, fairly, and impartially. As a mother, she wanted all of her children to feel equally loved. But there was something about her youngest, and their relationship, that made her heart soar whenever she thought about him. It made her happy to think about finding him a future, even as it made her heart ache to think he would move to another longhouse in another village. Perhaps a couple of miles to the east or west, if he joined the Turtle or Wolf Clans of their tribe. Or maybe much farther away if he joined another tribe. Though it might take several years, helping Wanders Far find his future had become her top priority.

Bear Fat was glad that Big Canoe asked a gifted spiritual leader to help with Wanders Far's rite of passage. After days of hiking, they were happy to finally reach the Moose River and put their canoes in the familiar water. Combining rivers, ponds, lakes, and portages along herd paths and game trails, they spent the next five days following the long-established route traveled by their friends, enemies, and ancestors. Wanders Far paddled the small canoe by himself. Big Canoe set the pace from the stern of the larger boat, a slow, steady, constant, rhythmic pace and Follows Stars adjusted his cadence at the bow. Bear Fat thought about the future, relaxed, and daydreamed, riding in the middle of the canoe. For such a hard-working woman, riding in the canoe while others worked was a rare luxury. Periodically she switched places with the seer, who whittled figurines and wooden bowls whenever he rode in the middle. They didn't talk much along the way. It was hard to talk in the canoe anyhow. Bear Fat liked to be able to see the face of the person she was talking to, rather than the back of a head.

At the end of the waterway, there was a fifteen-mile trek that led to their destination. The canoes were left hidden in the brush near the lake, and they set out on foot to their summer home.

About a week after they arrived, Follows Stars moved out of the camp at Copperas Pond, and he took Wanders Far with him. As he left, he told Big Canoe and Bear Fat that they would be near the top of the smaller mountain, just to the west of the giant mountain.

Follows Stars needed time alone with Wanders Far, as enjoyable as it was to spend time at Copperas Pond.

Follows Stars found a perfect place for his encampment near the apex of the little mountain. It afforded wonderful views to the east and the west, and also of the great mountain just above. They built a tiny, squat hut, not even big enough to stand up in, but long enough to fit 2, six-foot long bunks made of saplings. When that was done, they set up a fire pit a short distance from the opening to the hut, and then built a fire in the pit. It was a long day, and they accomplished a lot. At dark, they went to bed, and found the hut comfortable.

The next morning, Follows Stars sat across the fire from Wanders Far. Change was underway. They sat silently, looking into each other's eyes. They both knew it. Follows Stars began, "I have lots of questions for you, Wanders Far."

The boy replied, "Yes, Grandfather, I know."

Follows Stars was not a blood relative, but *grandfather* signified deference and respect. Wanders Far sat still and silent, patiently waiting for what came next.

Follows Stars nodded ever so slightly. Following a long pause, he slowly formed his first question. "Wanders Far, are you prepared to become a man and leave your boyhood behind you?"

"Yes, Grandfather, I am ready," Wanders Far replied matter-of-factly.

"Do you know the path you will follow?"

"Yes, Grandfather, I know the path I will follow. I will remain Wanders Far. I would follow my passion for traveling between our people's villages, carrying important messages. I believe that is the path the Great Spirit chose for me."

"Is that the only path you will follow, Wanders Far? Does the Great Spirit have other plans for you as well?"

"No, Grandfather, it is not the only path I will follow. The Great Spirit also has other plans for me, I understand that. I only know a little bit about that path."

Follows Stars let those words hang in the air between them for several moments. Then he asked, "Does the Great Spirit speak to you, Son?"

Wanders Far thought before answering slowly, "The Great Spirit does not speak to me in words. Sometimes I feel his spirit in my heart, and sometimes, I feel his power pass through me, through the air."

Follows Stars recalled, "Just like when we were at the Great Roaring Waterfalls? His spirit passed through you there, didn't it?"

"Yes, Grandfather," Wanders Far confirmed.

"You told me I had a glorious spirit," Follows Stars reminded. "I told you I was just about to say the same thing to you. Do you know I felt the power pass through me also that day?"

"Yes, I believe I did know that," Wanders Far confirmed.

Follows Stars asked, "Why do you think we both felt the Spirit pass through us?"

"It was meant to bring us together, Grandfather."

"Yes," Follows Stars agreed, "I think so too. Why do you think the Great Spirit has crossed our paths?"

"I am meant to follow you. You are meant to lead me, or guide me, or teach me. Maybe there is more."

Follows Stars nodded affirmation, then switched directions. "Do you have visions, Wanders Far? Do you see scenes in your head that you can't fully explain or understand?"

"Yes, Grandfather. I have visions. Sometimes I think I understand them, other times, I think I am meant to contemplate. I think I am meant to understand other visions later."

"How do the visions make you feel, Wanders Far?"

"Perhaps I feel honored to have these visions. I understand it might lead to great responsibility, or sacrifice. I am not afraid. I will follow the path I am destined to follow, Grandfather."

"Do you see the future? Do you know what is going to happen before it happens, Son?"

"Sometimes I see the future, but not very often. Sometimes I visualize the future and it happens just like I picture it. Sometimes I just know what will happen, without a vision of it. However, a lot of things happen that I have no vision of."

Follows Stars closed his eyes and pondered his next question. Was it too soon to ask? He decided it was time, and said, "Have you walked the earth before, Wanders Far?"

The boy nodded, and answered, "Yes, Grandfather, I believe I have. I believe I have walked the earth many times. I believe some of my visions are memories from when I have walked the earth before."

"Are your memories pleasant, happy memories, or are they gruesome, horrible, miserable memories?"

"Both," Wanders Far answered. A tear sprung from his eye and rolled down his stoic face. "Mostly I experience the memories as a vision, without emotions attached. Some of the visions are glorious, and some are horrific." He continued with a whisper that trailed off, "Sometimes I feel an emotion with the vision, but not very often."

"You just had a vision from a past life, accompanied by an emotion of sadness, didn't you, Wanders Far," the seer suggested.

"Yes, Grandfather, I had a vision of death, of a man I loved deeply. Maybe he was my father. He wore a dark brown robe, had no hair on his head, except for a little above his ears. He had blue eyes, and very pale skin. Many of my visions have these pale skinned people. Anyway, the spirit of this man reminded me of your spirit, Grandfather."

Follows Stars nodded. "Yes, I understand. I think it was me. I believe I have guided you in previous lives. I also believe one day you will guide me. Our paths cross often, Son. Is it your destiny to be a seer, Wanders Far?"

Wanders Far sat silent for a long time. Follows Stars waited for the answer to his question. It took over ten minutes before the boy voiced, "I cannot see whether it is my destiny to be a seer as well, but I see that I am a runner."

"Is it your destiny to be a healer?"

Wanders Far answered similarly.

"Is it your destiny to be a leader?"

Wanders Far concluded, "I will follow the path I was meant to follow. I know I am a runner. I may have opportunities to serve as a seer, a healer, or a leader, but I cannot clearly see those paths now."

Follows Stars asked softly, "Tell me about your dreams of flying."

Wanders Far closed his eyes and told about his experience with the foul tempered eagle two years earlier. His voice grew louder. His words came faster. He expressed great joy at soaring above the earth, gliding gently over the lake, and the sight of land in the distance, and then the heart-pounding excitement of the eagle's swift pursuit of the rabbit. Then Wanders Far talked about the spirit of the eagle.

Follows Stars was quiet for a minute, then he said, "When you speak of flying, far from the ground and far from the land, you sound happy and free. You say you will accept the destiny chosen for you, but it sounds like you would rather not be burdened."

Wanders Far hung his head. He didn't say anything. He didn't need to admit that Follows Stars was right.

Follows Stars continued, "Soon you will have to choose. It will be tempting to turn your back on Spirit. I don't know how you will choose."

Abruptly, Wanders Far interrupted. It hurt him that his guide did not trust him, yet he also felt uncertainty. How could he deny it?

Follows Stars repeated, "Soon you will have to choose. Your choice will have great consequences. The Great Spirit has beckoned. A dark spirit also haunts you. It knows your weakness. You have crossed its path before. It was following you on the wings of the eagle. It never expected your spirit to join it in flight. It wasn't ready for you then. It is ready for you now. You will face this spirit in other forms. I would like to warn you further, but this is all I know to tell you."

They sat quietly together for over an hour. Then Follows Stars asked, "Is your family aware of the things you have told me today, Son?"

"No," Wanders Far answered. "I haven't told anyone about my visions, but my mother looks at me strangely. Sometimes lately, I can read her thoughts. She understands I have visions, but she can't convert that understanding into words or questions. I think she knows I can read the thoughts of other people also. Not everybody—I don't pick the people whose thoughts I can read. They just come to me. Some people whose thoughts I can read, I stay far away from. I mostly seem to be able to read people's thoughts at a close distance. And my sister... I think Squash can see into my soul sometimes."

"Can you read my thoughts, Wanders Far?" Follows Stars asked.

"No, I can read your spirit, but I can't read your thoughts, Grandfather."

Follows Stars questioned, "Do you have the power to control people or animals with your presence?"

Wanders Far thought long before answering. He seemed to recall times as an infant when his spirit flew with tiny birds. Whatever he wished them to do, they did, swimming about the sky performing entertaining acrobatics for his amusement. It was hard to know whether that was a memory, or a childish fantasy. Otherwise, Wanders Far told Follows Stars that his ability seemed to be limited to sensing, feeling, observing, and suggesting. It hadn't occurred to him that his spirit could potentially control the action of others.

Follows Stars told Wanders Far that it probably was not possible, and if it were possible such power should be used very carefully. He ended their talk by repeating his warning about the dark spirit. "It knows your weakness."

Though it was still morning, both men were exhausted from the conversation. "We have much work to do, Wanders Far, but I must rest first." Follows Stars returned to the hut and lay down.

Wanders Far stood up to see him off. Then he spread his arms wide, tilted his head back, and stretched his fingers wide apart from each other, palms facing up. The mountain was right before him. The grass and trees were a bright, emerald green. The sky was baby blue. There were no clouds to be seen, and warm, comforting sunshine soaked through his skin. He was glad to be standing, and to feel his body awakening to the sensations of a new morning. It was time to stretch his legs.

An idea came to him. Why not climb the mountain? All the way to the top. Though he couldn't think of any reason to do it, he couldn't think of any reason not to either. It wasn't far from where they were, and moments after the impulse came to him, Wanders Far was on his way. For a while the going was difficult, due to the dense growth of forest and the steep terrain. Eventually Wanders Far found a game trail that seemed to be going in the right direction.

The tall pines gave way to shorter, twisted trees. Then he came around a corner and caught a glimpse of a deer in a small clearing. Unlike any he had seen before, the deer was pure white, not the buckskin color of most deer. He was a magnificent looking specimen, maybe 2-years-old, a good size, probably just reaching his peak weight and strength. Wanders Far froze in his tracks and quietly observed for over an hour. The stag didn't seem to have a care in the world. Wanders Far thought of the time when he and his grandmother froze in their tracks to watch a doe, five years earlier on the path to the waterfall at the foot of the mountain. The stag lifted his head from the grass he had been grazing on and turned to look in Wanders Far's direction. The deer had pink antlers and blue eyes. He was standing above Wanders Far on the trail and the white coat contrasted brilliantly against the powder-blue sky behind him. Though it was only early spring, his antlers were already impressive, and Wanders Far wondered what they would look like by the end of the summer. The deer's chest muscles were extraordinarily prominent for a deer, most likely from following the steep trail up and down the side of the mountain several times every day.

Then a jackrabbit caught sight or wind of Wanders Far and bounded off, creating a disturbance that set the white deer off. The great white stag crashed through the densely wooded trees on the opposite side of the clearing and Wanders Far could hear him for a couple of minutes, as the deer made his way back to a game trail. "It was a pleasure to meet you, friend," Wanders Far muttered.

A short distance farther along, Wanders Far left the last of the trees behind him. He picked his way up across the bare, rocky top of the mountain, sometimes scrambling on all-fours as he climbed to the topmost point. Then he stood on the top, crossed his arms across his chest, and slowly soaked it in.

He couldn't believe he had never made that climb before, after coming to visit the mountain every year of his life. Slowly he turned to enjoy a slightly different view in each direction. Again, he thought of his grandmother and the day they paddled around the figure-eight-shaped lake, with its two large islands. He held up his hand in front of his face and covered the lake with his left thumb, amazed at how small it looked from the top of the mountain. A couple of small, fluffy clouds floated beneath him, and Wanders Far was amazed to think he was looking at the top of a cloud. The cool spring air was colder still on the top of the mountain, but it was late morning, and the bright and brilliant sun warmed his bare skin in spite of the cool air. Wanders Far found a boulder and made himself comfortable. There was no reason to hurry back down the mountain.

Two hours later, Follows Stars joined Wanders Far on top of the mountain. Wanders Far watched as the seer surveyed the spectacular scene at his feet. It made Wanders Far happy to see the joy on the old man's face. He sat down on the large boulder next to Wanders Far, and they sat in silence for over an hour.

Then Follows Stars said, "Just because you see a little, doesn't mean you know it all, Wanders Far. In all my years, sometimes I think I have seen it all, but I haven't ever seen anything so spectacular as this! You have a very special gift, Son, and you must be very careful about sharing your gift with others. Sometimes your gift will be a treasured thing. Other times it will feel like a curse. You see a little, you think you know the rest, only you don't always. You will have to learn how to interpret your own visions, and always be careful not to draw too distant a conclusion. Although I have told you this, Wanders Far, you will make mistakes. Maybe some mistakes can be avoided. Will you remember this advice?"

Wanders Far nodded and told the seer that he would endeavor to remember.

Follows Stars gave an example. "I see some very sad times ahead for our people. A great sickness will come, and more than half of our people will die. Only I don't know if it will come this year, or a hundred years, or even a thousand years from now. What should I tell our people?"

Wanders Far turned to face the old man, a look of concern on his face. "I don't know. If the people knew, maybe they could do something to avoid the sickness. Maybe they could prepare. Or maybe they would panic. Maybe they would waste their lives worrying about something that might never happen. They might feel hopeless." He turned away looking back out over the expansive view below. Then he hung his head and concluded, "You should not share that vision yet."

After another long silence, Follows Stars asked, "Can you tell when a man's heart is true? When he is lying to you? Can you tell good from evil? Are our people good or evil?"

Wanders Far's eyebrows lowered and his chin hit his chest. Uncharacteristically he snapped, "Of course our people are good. Why would that be a question?"

They had a long discussion about their enemies, the necessity to defend their people from their enemies, the way their people attacked their enemies in retaliation and in provocation, the way they treated captives, and the way they treated casualties. Did their warriors' terrifyingly brutal acts minimize casualties by deterring the enemies' attacks on their people's villages? Why raid enemy villages and steal their property rather than work to secure the same resources with hard work? If you could kill one person and save many people by doing so, would it be a good thing to do? Follows Stars determined from the conversation that Wanders Far had an adult's understanding of how the world worked, the culture of their people, the political reality of life in their warrior society, and the danger of a world full of enemies.

A short break allowed for a change of direction. They sat cross-legged facing toward the east. Beyond the mountains there was a huge lake, not wide but very long, hundreds of miles long. Follows Stars had to squint to be sure it was a distant lake and not cloud cover. After a long look into the distance, Wanders Far closed his eyes and said, "That lake is to become important. People will fight to the death over that lake. Our people will meet a powerful new enemy there someday. We must be stronger before then. A new leader will unite us. I will carry his messages. His time has come. It is the will of the Great Spirit. Change is in the wind." Wanders Far opened his eyes and concluded, "Our people will know hard times, but good times too. We can help."

Wanders Far turned to face the old seer instead of the distant lake. "I want to tell you about something that happened today, Grandfather." He told Follows Stars about the great white stag. The old man listened intently, both to the facts and details of the encounter, and for the impression the encounter made upon the boy. He asked, "What does it mean?"

"It is significant. We shall see what it means." Follows Stars turned a little farther until they were sitting cross-legged, facing each other, knees touching. He reached forward for Wanders Far's hands, putting them together, palm to palm, and engulfed the boy's hands within his own. "Close your eyes, Son. Let us be silent." For twenty minutes, two powerful old souls wandered freely together between and within the conscious and subconscious hearts and minds of the old man and the boy.

Follows Stars opened his eyes. In a deep voice, he said slowly, "It is time, Wanders Far. Are you ready?"

"Yes, Grandfather, I am ready."

They made their way down from the summit of the mountain. Wanders Far gathered wood for the old man's fire. Follows Stars brought the morning fire back from embers and prepared a light meal. It would be the last meal for the boy before his long fast. At dusk they ate in silence. After dinner, Follows Stars told Wanders Far what would happen next. "This is a time for you to be silent. Absolutely quiet. I will give you limited instructions. Focus inward. Be aware of what you think, how you feel, what you 'see' and what you experience. We will sit together here for several hours. Then you will sleep. At dawn you will climb back to the summit, alone. You must go in silence. You must not utter a sound. Even your feet on the ground must travel the path as quietly as possible. You will take a blanket, and a pouch of water. You will spend three days and three nights at the summit. On the morning of the fourth day, you will return here to my fire. We will join hands together again. Then we will share a meal, and after that we will talk." The old man was quiet for a long time, just sitting quietly by the fire. Then he began to hum. Humming gave way to a chant. Periodically he tossed various aromatics into the fire. Some were subtle, some were extraordinarily pungent. Some smelled good and some smelled awful. Some popped, crackled, and made little explosions. Some caused profuse billowing smoke and some unnaturally changed the color of the flames. The old man's chants became louder and deeper, rhythmic, and intense. He moved around the fire in circles, dancing around, turning and twisting his old body, swinging his arms around below the levels of his knees, bending over at the waist, almost as if he were a wild animal on all fours. Hours later when it was over, Follows Stars rubbed Wanders Far's back, chest, face, and hair with a gloppy salve made from dried sage, mint leaves, and oil, and led him to his bunk in the hut.

At dawn, Follows Stars stirred cold black charcoal from the previous night's fire into bear oil to form a thick black paste. He dipped his left hand in the mixture, then he pressed his hand over Wander's Far's right eye. Follows Star's black thumbprint stood out on the middle of Wanders Far's forehead, his fingers made parallel lines between his forehead and his right ear, and the palm of his handprint covered Wanders Far's eye-socket. He stood back for a moment, like an artist surveying his handiwork. He nodded his head and grunted, pleased with himself.

Then Follows Stars handed Wanders Far his blanket, and a pouch of water, and pointed toward the summit of the mountain. He watched as the boy walked up the path, tiptoeing in silence. When he had disappeared from sight, Follows Stars returned to his bunk, still exhausted from the night before, and suffering from a powerful ache at the small of his back.

The first day on the mountain was carefree. Wanders Far tried to sit solemnly with his legs crossed as he waited to become enlightened. The spectacular scene beneath him was distracting. There was almost no breeze, and warm spring sunshine filled the world as far as his eyes could see. By mid-day, abundant sunshine directly overhead caused the surfaces of the rivers, streams, and brooks below to sparkle, silver and white, and the surfaces of the hundreds of small ponds and lakes reflected light back to the sun. As the day progressed, he changed his position hundreds of times, trying to lock the view from each direction firmly in his photographic mind.

By late afternoon, Wanders Far had grown tired of sitting. He had the feeling that his body should be moving, not frozen in silence. His instructions had been clear, he must remain perfectly quiet. He was not required to remain perfectly still. As quietly as possible he stood to his feet, stretched his arms and legs, and felt happy to be moving. He did hundreds of squat thrusts as silently as he could. He felt the blood moving through his body. He did sit-ups and push-ups until he felt like he might enjoy sitting silently again. Instead of sitting, Wanders Far decided to do some walking. He understood that he was to remain on the top of the mountain, so he resisted the urge to hike down to the big lake and back. He followed the ridge-line on top of the mountain from one end to the other, as far as he could go, and then back again. As he walked, Wanders Far thought about the day before, replaying his time with Follows Stars, and the ceremony he performed.

The hours passed more quickly as he walked the mountain top, and gradually the sunny day darkened to dusk, then to night. The moon was full and bathed the top of the mountain in soft moon-light. Wanders Far's spirit soared to see the expansive night sky, full of stars, from the top of the world in the middle of the night. He climbed to the highest point, lay down on his back with his knees bent, and looked up into the sky. He lay still for hours and gazed at the stars, so relaxed, he felt like his body had melted into the cold rock beneath him.

Near the middle of the night, the moon was overhead. He looked directly at the full moon, and then finally, a vision came. He felt a rush of adrenaline as the blood rushed through his body. Goosebumps spread across his chest and arms. All of a sudden, the moon trans-formed and encircled the face of a beautiful young woman, smiling, laughing, and looking directly into his eyes. Her long black hair blew from the wind at her face, swirling around behind her head. Her lips moved and he heard her soft, sweet voice say, "We were meant to be together, you and me, Wanders Far." He looked into her round eyes, and she continued to smile. Then all at once, she was gone, and in her place, the full moon returned to the sky. Wanders Far blinked, rubbed his eyes, then sat up, enjoying the memory of the vision of the beautiful girl. The scene repeated in his mind countless times. He couldn't sleep. He felt elated and miserable at the same time, joyful that she had come to him, and miserable to be separated from her. Wanders Far couldn't wait to meet the Moon Girl in the flesh.

Finally, he managed to doze off shortly before dawn and slept briefly, but long enough to have a dream of the same beautiful girl. Wanders Far awoke as the sun was rising, casting beams of light from over the top of the long lake to the east. He remembered the dream that came to him while he slept, of his Moon Girl, hand-feeding black-eyed Susans and purple coneflowers to timid, twin, spotted fawns, by a sandy beach on the shore of small lake.

The sun warmed the air, and he was lucky to get a second warm spring day on the top of the mountain. He was happy and he fantasized about building a longhouse on top of the mountain but understood that the top of a mountain was often inhospitable, with fierce, wintery weather sometimes even in the summer. During the second day, his stomach began to protest having been neglected. He thought of his grandmother, who always tried so hard to get him to eat more. He had saved his bag of water, using only enough to gently wet his lips and moisten his mouth the day before.

He spent most of the second day moving, with very little time sitting still. If he had counted, he might have made a thousand trips from one end to the other, not minding a single step. He had hoped for many more visions of the young woman. Instead, many strange scenes filled his mind, and he endeavored to remember each one. He knew that Follows Stars would want to hear every detail he could remember.

Wanders Far's mind wandered while he paced, and he had a

vision of a man named Two River Currents Flowing Together. Two Rivers visited the people, from village to village, talking to everyone about joining together in a great unification, a confederacy of tribes. He was unable to speak words properly, due to a stutter. Two Rivers was not able to persuade the people to listen.

When he came to the village where the People's River met the North River, Two Rivers climbed the tallest tree and instructed the men of the village to chop it down. He wanted to prove the power of his message, the truth in his words, and the support of the Great Spirit. When the tree fell, he was lost in the river, and none of the people were surprised. The next morning when everyone awoke, they found him sitting by a campfire in the middle of their village. The people were so impressed, they became the founding members of the confederacy.

Two Rivers traveled to the village with a man named He Who Seeks the Wampum Belt. Seeks Wampum was a traveling story-teller, and people enjoyed listening to him. Two Rivers was the great, visionary peacemaker, the planner, the originator of ideas. Seeks Wampum spoke the words, told the stories, and convinced the people to join the confederacy. As a powerful orator, he made music out of words, and even the sound of his name, in their native language, had a beautiful ring to it: Hiawatha.

Then, in his vision, Wanders Far observed the two men traveling together along the People's River and Wanders Far also saw that he *himself* was traveling with them. Then he saw they approached his home village at Garoga Creek. Then in the daydream he saw the three of them together at a Women's Council meeting, after which Wanders Far left Garoga Creek by himself. He saw that he was to become a runner between villages and tribes, carrying their message of unification, and calling councils to participate in a great gathering. Wanders Far noticed that he was not older in the vision. Those events were not in the distant future. Perhaps they were just about to happen.

Wanders Far's heart warmed at the realization. He *was* a runner!

Later in the afternoon, still pacing, another strange vision played out in his mind. It was the terrible sickness that Follows Stars spoke about. He could see the village of his people however it wasn't in the same location. The village had moved, and Wanders far was familiar with that location, a couple miles to the north of their present village. He didn't specifically recognize any of the people in the vision, but somehow, he understood them to be from his village. He floated through the village, from one longhouse to the next, and the scene was the same in each one. The people were very sick from spotted, scabby, pus-infested rashes. Most of the infirm lay on their bunks. Most of them were adults and older children. Very few of the elderly or youngest children and babies managed to survive. A few of the survivors who were no longer sick tended to the needs of the others. He noticed that the contents of the households included lots of implements that looked strange to him. He was saddened by the thought that this could happen to his people, and he understood the dilemma that Follows Stars wrestled with. Could they find any way to avoid that outcome? Given the strange things he noticed inside the longhouses, and since he didn't recognize any of the people specifically, he guessed that the vision was in a distant future time.

From the top of the mountain, Wanders Far looked to the southwest. He could see some of the route they traveled from their home at Garoga Creek. And then another vision came to him. Many of the rivers they used to travel north to the mountains had been turned into enormous connected lakes. Paddling the lakes was a lot easier than paddling the river, and the new lakes were beautiful. He saw the devices that caused the rivers to become lakes. Dams made of manmade rock caused the rivers to back up, and Wanders Far thought of the beavers, nature's dam builders, and he wondered at the power of a people who could build rocks and turn rivers into lakes. He thought about the work it took to make the tiny dam at Garoga

Creek and imagined the effort it would take to make an enormous lake rather than a tiny swimming hole.

A couple of hours later, Wanders Far had a vision of an enormous settlement at the junction of the two rivers: The People's River and the North River. Instead of a village, or a couple of villages, there were more houses than he could count. Strange looking houses. Tall squares, rather than long rectangles, and some reached high up into the sky. There were ribbons of rock that looked like rivers, but they weren't made of liquid. In his vision, from high above, looking down, strange little squares zipped around on the surface of the ribbons of rock, and from a closer distance, he saw that the strange little squares contained people, those pale-skinned people he had often seen in visions. That particular vision seemed like it must be very far in the future. He saw some people with darker-colored skin as well but didn't notice people that looked like his people.

After dark, Wanders Far had a vision of his people in a different settlement. They were high up in the sky, sitting on silver logs, having a meal, fearlessly dangling their legs over the edge. One wrong move, and they'd fall fast to their deaths below. It was one of those strange buildings, like a longhouse, only tall, and made of shiny materials instead of wood. It appeared to be on an island by a giant river, the biggest river he had ever seen, and it dumped into the biggest lake he had ever seen, a lake that he could not see the end of. Perhaps it was a lake so big that it should be called something else. He also observed that his people were dressed strangely, very different than he was accustomed to seeing. He couldn't help but notice that one of the young men looked exactly like his older brother Chipmunk, and he thought about his brother scampering around on the top of their own longhouse when they were younger.

It was another chilly night on the mountain. Wanders Far was able to find a soft spot among some sedges, moss, and lichens on a dry patch of dirt, somewhat protected from the chilly wind. He wrapped himself in his blanket, curled himself up into a fetal position, and slept for several hours, recalling no dreams when he awoke at sunrise.

It looked like Wanders Far's was going to get three consecutive pleasant spring days on the mountain, until the sunrise gradually gave way to increasing cloud cover. From the top of the mountain, he saw the clouds gathering mass as they approached from the west. He could see it was going to get nasty on the top of that mountain, and the bad weather came fast.

For a while, he was able to appreciate the strange beauty of the dark clouds swallowing up the view beneath him. He felt wisps of clouds pass through him, engulfing him briefly, then passing by. He felt as "one" with the mountain, standing firm against the onslaught, determined to remain standing after it passed. The temperature plummeted. Wanders Far found cover beneath a boulder perched on top of three other boulders, which formed a natural shelter. He wrapped himself in his blanket and sat under the giant rock, enduring the biting wind and avoiding the worst of the penetrating rainfall. It wasn't long until the rain solidified into freezing rain, then snow. Wanders Far clenched his teeth, opened his lips as wide as he could, baring his teeth to the miserable weather, daring it to do its worst. If he hadn't committed to total silence, he might have growled or even roared. It was a part of the challenge. He would face it like a warrior.

His mind wandered. Another vision came to him. It was a vision of a giant canoe, a boat that looked like it had bare trees growing from the top of it, and had giant wings tied into the branches. That boat was in the lake that he saw from the top of the mountain, the one he and Dandelion explored with Blue Arrow, off to the east. He saw some of the men getting out of that boat and dropping into a smaller one that took them to the shore. Then he saw a battle between them and a party of his people. Three of his people died, and the rest quickly vanished into the woods. The pale-skinned people had a weapon that made loud noises and sent explosions from the end of their weapons. The men on the boat called their leader by the name of Champlain. Wanders Far came to understand through his vision that Champlain would give his name to that lake.

Another vision which seemed connected to the first vision, and yet disconnected at the same time, featured a man on a giant boat with wings. He saw that boat slowly cross a huge body of water and enter a river far wider than the People's River. He recognized that river from his previous vision of the giant shiny buildings on the island at the mouth of the river. Only there were no giant shiny buildings on the island in the vision he was having at that moment. The boat continued up the river. Wanders Far was surprised to see that river was the same one that became the North River. The boat went as far as the village where the peacemaker and the orator, Two Rivers and Seeks Wampum, began the unification. The place where Two Rivers fell from the giant tree into the river before disappearing overnight.

Wanders Far's vision revealed the leader of the pale-skinned people on the boat, a man that the others called Hudson. He could see that Hudson and his men carried the same fire-stick weapons that Champlain's men carried. At the village of his people, Hudson and his men disembarked from their boat. He saw them attempting to communicate with the people and managing to negotiate a trade of skins and furs for some of the unusual items Wanders Far had seen in other visions. The encounter with Hudson ended far better than the encounter with Champlain.

Wanders Far momentarily became aware of his cold and windy surroundings on the top of the mountain, and then his vision of Hudson continued. There was a boy with him and perhaps the boy was almost old enough to be a man. The boat wasn't in the same river, but rather on a large lake. The boat was frozen to the lake, and it looked like it had been stuck there for many months. His vision moved in fast-forward, until the lake had melted, and the boat floated freely on the surface of the lake. He could see and hear the men arguing in a strange language. A large group of men physically overpowered the leader and put Hudson, his son, and a couple of other men on a small boat. The large group of men sailed away in the big boat. Hudson tried to keep up with the other boat as best he could, until he couldn't keep up any longer. It was hopeless. They had been abandoned there. The vision led quickly to the unfortunate demise of that small group of men as they were met by a party of Algonquins the instant they attempted to put their feet on land. The Algonquins were pleased with the boat and fire-sticks they had taken possession of. Otherwise, the resources they secured were quite meager. It didn't look like Hudson, his son, or any of his men survived.

The storm on the top of the mountain was bone-chillingly miserable. He had been huddled and shivering for hours, and he couldn't sit any longer. There was just enough room under the roof of rock for him to jump up and down. He did that for a while and it felt good to move around. Quietly as he could, without so much as a grunt, he did as many squats, sit-ups, and push-ups as he could endure. Then he hopped from one foot to the next to keep his body temperature up. Fortunately, Wanders Far had the stamina to do so for several hours.

Just after dark, the storm that punished the summit of the ancient mountain ended the way it began. Wanders Far sat silently observing, and to his amazement, standing twenty-five feet from him, was the great white stag, who appeared from the mist of the dissipating storm clouds, unflinching, not moving even the slightest muscle, as if he were frozen. The higher-level clouds dissolved into the air first, exposing the stars and the moon, which shined down from the heavens, illuminating the snow that covered the peak of the mountain and the dark grey puffs of clouds that hovered below, down at the level of the tree line. The deer was still standing there when once again the pretty girl's face appeared, framed by the moon. She said, "You know the path you must follow. You will find me along the way." Then she repeated what she had said on the first night. "We were meant to be together, you and me, Wanders Far." She smiled sweetly, turned her head, and was gone.

Wanders Far stared longingly at the moon for an hour after that. He took a long drink of water, then huddled under his blanket, hoping to generate warmth from his own breath under its cover. He didn't sleep. He had no more visions. He tried to force his body not to be cold. No matter what position he tried, he couldn't get warm, but he managed to survive a night that seemed to last a week. Finally, the sun rose over Champlain's lake to the east. He wanted to jump up and down for joy, beat his fists on his chest, and proclaim for all the world in his loudest warrior voice, that he was a man, and he had survived the mountain.

He stood on the top of the mountain facing the rising sun, head tilted back, arms stretched wide, and his head facing the sky above. A brown hawk soared toward him, gliding slowly and gracefully from the east. Wanders Far wondered if the hawk would land on his outstretched arm. Instead it landed at his feet. Wanders Far didn't move. The beady eyes of the hawk met the boy's gaze.

Wanders Far heard a soft deep voice question, "Will you ride with me this morning, friend?"

Wanders Far nodded.

Moments later, Wanders Far was gliding around the summit of the tall mountain, completing a full circle. Then the hawk flew farther away. The soft deep voice asked, "Would you like to go farther still?" Wanders Far nodded again. An hour later the voice asked again. Wanders Far shook his head. It was time to return. He had been gone too long as it was. The voice suggested an adventure so grand that it sounded unbelievable. The voice spoke of magical places Wanders Far couldn't imagine. Wanders Far shook his head no again. The hawk returned to the mountain. Wanders Far saw his body standing on the top of the mountain, just as he had left it. The hawk landed on his left arm, and Wanders Far's spirit returned to his body. He nodded, a gesture symbolizing his gratitude for the gift of flight that morning. The flight had been even more breathtaking than his previous experience. He appreciated a more welcoming host.

As the hawk disappeared onto the horizon, Wanders Far's thoughts returned to his mountain quest. It was time to return to camp. As he started down from the mountain, he thought of the deer.

The great white stag had not been a vision. Wanders Far knew that for certain because he followed the trail that the stag had left in the snow on the way down from the summit of the mountain. Wanders Far walked slowly and slouched so that if he slipped on the snow or ice, he wouldn't fall hard. Fortunately, the tracks led him safely down to the tree line and the game trail that Wanders Far was familiar with. He was mighty glad to smell the smoke of Follows Stars' fire. Follows Stars had a warm herbal tea and some hot, thick soup ready for him. As Wanders Far approached, Follows Stars held his index finger up to his lips, indicating that the silence should continue. Wanders Far drank the tea and ate half of the soup as quietly as he could. Then Follows Stars pointed to the hut. Wanders Far went in, laid down on his bunk, and slept until noon.

It was a nice spring day, but Follows Stars kept the fire burning strong nonetheless. He sat by the fire and watched the entrance to the hut, until Wanders Far came out. When Wanders Far finally emerged from the hut, something seemed different about him. The old man couldn't tell exactly what it was. He gestured, and Wanders Far sat across the fire and silently waited.

Follows Stars emptied a pouch full of dried leaves and twigs on the fire. The flames turned blue and the air smelled like cedar, mushrooms, and rotting logs. Then he sat in front of Wanders Far, just as he had before, knees to knees, his knobby, wrinkled hands wrapped around Wanders Far's. Follows Stars closed his eyes and Wanders Far did the same. Wanders Far felt a deep connection to the old man in front of him. He was happy to sit there, and in no hurry to be anywhere else.

When he was ready, Follows Stars opened his eyes and softly said, "Wanders Far, you may speak now."

Wanders Far opened his eyes, put his hands on his knees, sat forward, and said evenly, "It is good to see you again, Father."

"I am glad you are well, Wanders Far. Tell me everything about your experience. Leave nothing out. I will not speak until you are done."

Wanders Far did as instructed, telling Follows Stars about the ascent, the weather, the beautiful view, what it looked like at sunrise and at sunset, the terrible storm, and the visions. He retold the visions in order, starting and ending with the pretty woman in the moon, the flight with the hawk, the story of Two Rivers and Seeks Wampum, his vision of the great sickness, the appearance of the lakes where the rivers had been previously, the big city at the junction of the two rivers, the skyscrapers and the role of the people in building them, and the stories of the explorers, Champlain, and Hudson. It took four hours to tell. He didn't leave anything out, and perhaps shared even more detail about his own feelings and thoughts about the visions than Follows Stars might have expected.

Follows Stars asked, "You left one vision out of your story, didn't you, Brother?"

Wanders Far looked down at his ankles and a tear rolled down each cheek. "I did," Wanders Far admitted.

Follows Stars reassured him, "It is okay, I have seen it also, and

I know the time is near. I am ready to rejoin the spirit world, and someday you will join me there too. It is a good day to die."

Their conversation then became light-hearted and relaxed, no longer the formal exchange between wise sage and prized pupil. Follows Stars said, "I have some gifts for you, just a few things I'd like you to have." Follows Stars handed Wanders Far a wampum belt and said, "When you return to Garoga Creek, take this belt to your sister, the one you call Squash, and ask her to tell you what it means." Then he handed Wanders Far a pouch and told him that he could open it back at Copperas Pond. "Just a little something I whittled up for you while you were up on the mountain top." Wanders Far stood silently for a moment, surprised to receive a gift from his mentor. He had few physical possessions. He bowed his head slightly, an expression of his gratitude. Then they enjoyed a relaxing dinner by the fire and went to bed early.

At dawn, Wanders Far tried to wake the old man. They had planned to leave at first light. Wander's Far put his hand on the old man's shoulders and shook him gently, and then more vigorously. Follows Stars opened his eyes, and said, "You have a glorious spirit, Wanders Far." Then he took his last breath. Wanders Far dropped to his knees. He turned his head sideways on the old man's chest. It was still, and Wanders Far couldn't hear a heartbeat.

Of course he had known that the time was near. Both men had felt it. Both had foreseen it. Still, Wanders Far had thought perhaps that it might yet be weeks or months in the future. In their warrior society, *It is a good day to die* was kind of a motto, or mantra, usually not something to be taken literally.

Less than two minutes after Follows Stars took his last breath, Wanders Far felt the spiritual essence of the old seer's soul slowly levitate from his bunk. It was a thick, powerful force of energy, and Wanders Far could feel its presence far above the constraints of the twig and bark roof of the little hut. Wanders Far stepped out of the hut and still felt the slowly-rising spirit lifting dozens of feet above the hut, and then, in a flash of a moment, Follows Stars was gone.

Wanders Far knew that he should make a hasty descent. Follows Stars should be placed on a proper scaffold. He should be properly mourned. Wanders Far knew that he should bring his friend back to Copperas Pond. His mother and father would want to help.

Slowly and sadly, Wanders Far fashioned a travois. The travois was made from a couple of long sticks tied together to form a drag-gable stretcher. When he finished, he couldn't bear to leave. He sat on a boulder. He looked up to the sky. He whispered sadly, "How could you leave me?" There wasn't so much as a breeze. Nothing seemed to move, anywhere. He repeated his question, louder the second time, almost demanding an answer. He put his head in his hands and sobbed. An hour later he thought he couldn't cry any-more. He looked up to the sky and yelled. "How could you leave me! I have so much to learn. I can't do this on my own." Then he sobbed some more. Their time together was brief, though intense. Wanders Far would have benefitted from more time with his guide. Though he knew he should start down the mountain with his friend's corpse, he curled up into a ball and slept.

When he woke up it was late afternoon. He saw the hawk perched on Follows Stars' chin. He jumped up, and shoed the bird away from the body.

"What are you doing," Wanders Far demanded instinctively. "Just look at me, talking to a stupid bird!" He shouted his self-ad-monishment as if he meant to share it with the Great Spirit.

The hawk answered. "Is that any way to speak to a friend?" It was the voice of Follows Stars, or at least it sounded like it.

Wanders Far rubbed his eyes in disbelief. He hadn't heard the voice in his head, in the realm of the spirit world. The bird's beak had opened, and he heard the words from outside his body. He felt foolish talking to the bird, but the bird's words were reassuring. The voice of his lost friend was comforting. It was strange to see his mentor's dead body there before him, yet sharing conversation with his spirit. The hawk told Wanders Far that it heard his message. It understood that Wanders Far wasn't ready for his destiny. It validated his self-doubts. "Let me fly you off to the world of spirits and we can soar freely together through the ages," it suggested.

Wanders Far protested, "I have to tend to your funeral. I have to take your body down the mountain and mourn you properly."

The hawk replied, "Just pitch my dead body in the gorge. You don't need your body anymore either. Our spirits long for freedom."

Wanders Far stood there, mouth open wide, amazed to think of the words he was hearing. He found the suggestion alluring and seductive. It didn't sound like anything Follows Stars would say, yet he heard every word. Finally he whispered, "Come back at dawn."

The rest of the day he moped around, wandering aimlessly. He thought he knew what he should do. The hawk's offer was tempting. Maybe his destiny was to deliver spirit messages through the sky rather than words and stories along the trail on land. All night he argued with himself. He doubted his own spirit. He pulled his hair to see if he could feel it. Was all of this a dream? He pulled harder. He cut his thigh with a shark rock. Beads of blood jumped to the surface of his skin. It was not a dream. He felt pain and he saw blood. He didn't sleep at all that night, and was in a foul mood in the morning when the hawk returned.

Wanders Far shouted, "You were the only one that really, truly understood me. I still needed you and then you had to die. Get lost!" With angry tears in his eyes, Wanders Far threw a heavy rock at the hawk and turned away. He had a duty to tend to.

At the front of the travois, Wanders Far held the sticks in his hands, and the sticks rode at his hips. He tried not to think any thoughts on the way down the mountain. They came anyway.

He had always done his best thinking while he was walking.

Suddenly it came to him. He remembered the words of Follows Stars before the quest: "Soon you will have to choose. It will be tempting to turn your back on Spirit. I don't know how you will choose." Had the dark spirit pretended to be Follows Stars? Hungry, thirsty, and tired, he had to admit to himself that he had reached his limits. He had almost thrown himself over the edge of the cliff to follow a dark spirit. The closer to Copperas Pond he got, the better he felt. "I've been tested, and I've passed the test. I will follow the path I am meant to follow." He finally felt like himself again with those words in his mind.

Wanders Far dragged the dead body of his spiritual guide, mentor, and friend, as well as his friend's possessions, all the way back down the mountain to Copperas Pond. The descent from the little mountain made for a long, sad funeral procession, and Wanders Far stopped several times. Wanders Far was accustomed to spending a lot of time alone, but on that day, he felt a deep, empty feeling of loneliness. Soon he would be in camp with his mother and father, enjoying their company, and happy in their warm presence, but not completely understood. Wanders Far felt like only Follows Stars had completely understood him. He would never forget the old seer.

Bear Fat and Big Canoe were alone together at Copperas Pond for the first time since they were married. While Wanders Far was away, they had worked on building a canoe. It was work best performed by at least two people, and they worked in close proximity to one another. There had been plenty of time to enjoy idle conversation as they worked at their craft.

Both of them had just turned 50-years-old. All three of their daughters were well into their thirties. Their three grown sons were all in their twenties. They were luckier than most families. It was rare for families to have that many children reach adulthood. They were grandparents many times over, and their first great-grandchild was expected soon. They felt fortunate to be in good health and Bear

Fat also felt lucky that her mother was still living and still healthy at 66-years-old. They were getting old, there was no denying that, but they remained solid contributors, providing essential resources for the people, and helping to lead, govern, and guide their tribe.

For a couple of years, Bear Fat had been thinking about transferring her role as head of household to one of the other women. She had been in charge of the longhouse and had served on the Women's Council for thirty years. She asked her husband, "What do you think?"

Big Canoe told his wife that she should continue in her role as leader. She did a great job, nobody ever complained, she was happy, healthy, and able, not to mention as pretty as the day they were married.

Bear Fat laughed at his conclusion. They had been happy throughout their marriage and remained happy still. "Couldn't I be a butt-ugly, beady-eyed possum, and still be a just and fair ruler of our village?" she protested. "Anyway, isn't it better for the future of our people to develop new leaders? Isn't it time for us to become tribal elders?"

Big Canoe replied, "Perhaps you're right, I guess, but when I look at you I don't see a tribal elder. Maybe your baby sisters, but not you," he joked. "Besides, who do you think could replace you?"

"I have given that a lot of thought. As you mentioned, my three sisters are old, like me. Of my six nieces, I've been watching the serious, industrious one—Robin's Egg. Then there are our three daughters. Sure, we love all of them, and we're proud of the lives they've built, and the women they have become. Objectively speaking, who would be the best choice?"

They discussed each of their daughters' strengths and weaknesses. Corn was like her grandmother, very loyal, dependable, hardworking, and caring. She also had her grandmother's wide-eyed, innocent sweetness. She never showed interest in metering out justice or guiding others in one direction or another. Her husband, Black Walnut, was chief of their Bear Clan. They had three sons and a daughter.

Bean was a gifted potter. The clay pots and bowls she made were works of art, far more attractive than the chunky, utilitarian pinch-pots used by many families. She was also great at making clothing from hides and furs. When it came to other work around the village, Bean often tried to get others to do her own share of the work. She and her husband had three daughters and two sons. Their oldest daughter was of marrying age, and Bear Fat mentioned as an aside that they would soon need to build a couple more compartments onto the end of their longhouse.

Getting the discussion back to succession, they discussed their third daughter, Squash. Squash was a weaver, artist, and historian. People came from great distances to tell her their stories, and if they brought enough clamshells, she would record their stories in woven, beaded, wampum belts. Squash was patient, loyal, hard-working, loving, and kind. She was a good teacher and provider. She shied away from confrontation, controversy, and telling people what they sometimes needed to hear. Squash's husband had been killed about a year earlier. He had been out hunting with the dog, Spirit. After Flint was killed by a rampaging moose, the dog disappeared, ending up at Cave Eye village. Blue Arrow was amazed to see the dog return to the village where she was born. He immediately set out to return the dog to Garoga Creek. Blue Arrow was a great comfort to Squash following the loss of her husband. It wasn't long before they married, and he once again became a replacement husband. Squash had two sons, 15 and 7-years-old. Squash's rambunctious baby girl, Somersault, was 3-years-old.

Big Canoe asked, "Has anyone expressed any interest in becoming the head of the household?"

Bear Fat looked up from stitching the birch bark to the cedar frame of the canoe, scratched her chin, and said, "That is an excellent question. Now that you mention it, the only one I can think of who has expressed any interest is Somersault!" They shared a hearty laugh. Already, precocious Somersault had shown signs of developing great leadership qualities.

Big Canoe was shaping the last of the ribs for the inside of the canoe. He stopped for a moment and thought out loud, "What if you got everyone together and told them what was on your mind? Our people participate in all kinds of decisions. Maybe someone has thought of something that you haven't thought of."

They agreed that it was an excellent idea. Bear Fat gave her husband a big kiss on her way to boil a pot of spruce gum. Before she got to the pot, she saw Wanders Far coming into camp and ran to help.

The canoe project was abandoned for the rest of the day. They built a scaffold between a couple of trees near the edge of the pond. Wanders Far made a modest fire beneath the scaffold. For the next ten days and nights, he maintained the fire, as dictated by custom. Because he thought Follows Stars would appreciate it, he frequently added a pinch or two of the dried powders from Follows Stars' collection.

Bear Fat helped Wanders Far go through the old seer's possessions, and they prepared most of the possessions for burial. Aside from the dried leaves and powders, there wasn't much to speak of: some blankets, clothes, his woodworking tools, a knife, a hatchet, and a digging tool made of bone. Wanders Far showed his mother the gift Follows Stars had given him—a collection of small wooden figurines. One depicted a young woman, and it took Wanders Far's breath away whenever he saw it. It looked exactly like the girl he saw in the moon on the mountain during his rite of passage. The second figurine was of a majestic deer. Follows Stars had found some way to dye the wood white, and the antlers had a subtle pink hue. It looked just like the great white stag that Wanders Far had encountered on the mountain. He hadn't realized that Follows Stars had seen it too. The third figure was a likeness of the old seer himself. Wanders Far liked to travel light, carrying as little as possible. Material things meant little to him. He did treasure the figurine of the runner that Follows Stars gave him at the Great Roaring Waterfalls, the two rocks from the race, and the bag of quartz crystals tied to his bunk. He would cherish the three new carvings as well.

During the mourning period, Wanders Far kept busy by burying the crystal necklaces in shallow holes underneath medium-sized rocks in various locations around the camp at Copperas Pond. He was surprised to find how much he enjoyed hiding the little gifts for the future. Wherever he found a strange little sheltered hiding spot, he placed a box in it. Many ended up in tiny crevices in rocky outcroppings along the various trails they traveled.

Follows Stars' body was removed from the scaffolding ten days after his death, and placed back on the travois. Big Canoe and Bear Fat joined Wanders Far in his ascent of the little mountain. Sometimes they needed to help lift the back of the travois to clear a steep incline. They found a perfect spot to bury the old seer's body and his possessions, not far from the fire pit where he performed Wanders Far's rite of passage ritual.

They spent the night in the hut Follows Stars and Wanders Far had built, and in the morning, Wanders Far convinced his parents to indulge in a trip up the mountain. It wasn't that much farther. They kept a good pace and made it to the top by mid-morning. Wanders Far was glad that he had insisted on leading them to the top of the mountain. It gave him great joy to see the look of wonder on his mother's face. They stayed for several hours. Bear Fat had never seen anything like it and had to survey the scenery from every vantage point three times before she was ready to descend. Big Canoe knew the mountain quite well from years of tracking and hunting bears, but never thought to stand on top of it. Big Canoe felt sheepish for not having brought Bear Fat to the top of the mountain himself, many years earlier.

The next day, they were back at the camp on Copperas Pond. The three of them worked quickly together to finish the new canoe, then enjoyed a swim and several jumps from the ledge.

After their swim, they gathered by the fire. With the mourning and burial complete, it was time for the family to recognize the new man in the family. The long, floppy mop of hair on Wanders Far's head had to be removed. One by one, Bear Fat plucked all of the hair from Wanders Far's head until all that remained was within a three-inch radius on the top, at the back of his head. Most men kept short locks there but Wanders Far asked to keep the hair at the topknot long. He sat quietly, teeth clenched, as silent as he had been on the top of the mountain. He would never have complained, but he was amazed that a tiny thing like hair plucking could be so painful. He sat motionless, through pluck after pluck, hour after hour. He was sure that the task wasn't any more pleasant for his mother. As was required, Wanders Far endured.

They hadn't spoken about Wanders Far's rite of passage. Bear Fat asked Wanders Far to tell her the story of his time on the mountain. Wanders Far told his mother most of the story. He shared his vision of Moon Girl, which seemed to interest his mother. He went into great detail about the three days on the peak of the mountain. Most of the more spiritual elements he kept to himself. He was not ready to talk freely about the claim Spirit had on his destiny. Bear Fat inquired about Follows Stars' reading. Wanders Far told her that they shared a special bond and a spiritual connection. Wanders Far told her that he was meant to be a runner and very possibly a seer as well. Perhaps even a healer. He ended by sharing, "On our giant mountain, it seems that He Who Follows the Stars became He Who Asks Many Questions, though he already knew the answers. It was such a gift to have someone in my life who completely understands me. I miss him terribly, and I will never forget him." Wanders Far smiled gratefully at his mother. She winked at him, and then plucked another hair.

After all the hairs had been removed, Bear Fat rubbed slippery, red-stained clay where the hair had been. Wanders Far found the slimy scalp massage soothing. The remaining hair was braided into tiny braid-strands, each in a slightly different style, and adorned with various natural decorations that Bear Fat had collected while Wanders Far was away on his quest. She stepped back to survey her work. Her wandering toddler suddenly looked like a warrior. Wanders Far had become a man.

Big Canoe and Wanders Far spent the next morning fishing. It was rare for them to be able to spend a morning alone together. They chatted comfortably along the short hike to the bountiful trout river from Copperas Pond. As they prepared their hooks and bait, Big Canoe told Wanders Far, "Son, I'm very proud of you. I always have been, and I always will be. Since you were born, I knew there was something special about you that I would never fully understand. You are smart in ways I can't comprehend. Whenever you are gone, wherever you go, always know that your mother and I love you, support you, and can't wait until we see you again. There's nothing more we want than for you to be happy, but we know you also have a destiny that calls for you. Walk tall, stand proud, and answer the call. I am absolutely confident that you will know what you need to do." Then Big Canoe placed his large hands on his son's shoulders, looked him dead in the eyes, and said, "Now let's put some fish on our hooks!"

Wanders Far was grateful and proud. Big Canoe wandered downstream and Wanders Far wandered upstream. They returned to camp just after midday with a huge pile of fish. Bear Fat helped them gut and clean the fish and hung most of them to dry on racks near the fire. Some of the fish and all of the waste was packaged into a bag.

After a quick lunch, Big Canoe and Wanders Far rubbed their bodies with some dank mud from the far end of Copperas Pond to disguise their human smells. They hoped to fool the mosquitos as well as the bears. Then they were back on the trail with a big smelly bag of bear bait.

They traveled up the mountain, following the same route that Big Canoe always used. Over the years he had established a dozen perfect spots to place the bait. That afternoon he decided to try his favorite spot, the one that had worked for him best throughout the years. He had stacked some wood and trees and left an opening to insert the bait. They scooped the smelly junk into the void and then continued along the trail. The trail went uphill from there and doubled back across a ridge that brought them to a perfect vantage point, downwind and high above the bait box. It was late afternoon, the perfect time for a hungry bear to have some dinner. Big Canoe set Wanders Far in the prime spot to draw a perfect bead on a bear at the bait. He instructed Wanders Far to sit, bow in hand, arrows at the ready. Then they waited.

A fairly small bear ambled up the path. He stopped at the bait box and ate for a while. Wanders Far looked at Big Canoe, who shook his head and whispered, "No."

About ten minutes later, a much larger bear walked up the same path and chased the smaller bear off the bait. Wanders Far looked at Big Canoe again. Big Canoe whispered, "Whenever you are ready, Son."

Wanders Far sent a fast arrow, straight and true, and it found its target right between the big bear's ribs, just behind his left foreleg, not far from his armpit. The bear took off running like it had been scared off by a ghost.

Big Canoe stood at the ready with a second arrow set on his bow. He put the arrow back in his quiver and put his arm around Wander's Far's shoulder. "Nice job," he said. "I guess we have yet another expert bear hunter in the family."

They followed the bear's path. It didn't take long to locate it. It managed to crash through the brush for a couple hundred yards. While the bear took its last breaths, Big Canoe set up a quick camp. Wanders Far sparked a fast fire from a piece of flint into a clump of dried moss. When the bear had finished bleeding out, they separated the skin from the carcass and butchered him. They filled their pack baskets with meat then quickly fashioned a travois. Then they wrapped the slabs of fat in the bearskin and tied it on to the travois. They took turns sleeping and watching for predators who might attempt to steal the bear overnight. In the morning they hauled the bear back to Copperas Pond.

While they were gone, Bear Fat had a visitor. When she was alone in camp, she liked to keep weapons ready in case she suddenly needed to mount a quick defense. She was sitting in the doorway of the wickiup, working on softening a small foxskin, when out of the corner of her eye she saw a medium sized bear approaching the trout that was drying on the racks less than twenty yards from where she sat. She carefully reached for a bow and stood up. She set up an arrow. The bear turned toward the rack and reached for a chunk of fish. She pulled the string and sent the arrow flying. It hit the bear in the same spot Wanders Far had hit his bear. The surprised bear crashed into Bear Fat's drying racks and sent the fish flying. He got his forearms caught in the drying racks and didn't have enough life left to dislodge himself. Then he died.

When Wanders Far and Big Canoe returned the next day with their bear, they were surprised to see a bearskin already staked out on the ground and bear meat slowly drying on the racks by the fire. Bear Fat looked up from her work, scraping the back of the bearskin to remove bits of meat and fat that clung to the skin. She set down her scraper and gestured with both arms toward her kill, then bowed proudly before walking to meet her husband and son.

"I guess you don't have to go all the way to the top of the mountain to find a bear," she joked. Big Canoe proudly complimented his wife and then he told her the story of Wanders Far's first successful bear hunt. They worked together to stake the second skin for cleaning. Bear Fat sprinkled salt on the hide, and then they took a break by the fire.

As they relaxed and chatted, meat bubbling in a stew pot, Bear Fat had a fleeting feeling. She wished she could freeze that moment in time. All of her other children had grown. She had spent part of the summer alone with her husband. Now her last child was grown also. Maybe next year he would be married and living far away. It made her sad to think of making the trip to Copperas Pond without any of her children in the years to come. It gnawed at her. "So be it," she thought, resigned to let the fates do what they would. She focused her energy on enjoying the last days of summer. Defiantly, she stood up, put her hands on her hips, and pointed at their bearskins. "Now we are all bear hunters!"

Chapter Eighteen
That Is How Your Story Should Be Told, My Friend

T hey returned home to big news.

The Women's Council hastily called a public meeting at the village center. Wanders Far listened as Bear Fat was told about two visitors who had just left the village earlier that day, and what they were suggesting. Wanders Far's heart raced, his jaw dropped, and blood rushed through his veins. The vision he had about the unification of tribes wasn't some far-off event. It was happening, right then and there. He listened intently to hear what the women were saying. Would they be in favor of the plan? It seemed like such an obvious choice to Wanders Far. One woman spoke against the proposal. The others seemed open to the idea, but not in any mood to make a hasty decision. Wanders Far knew it was time for him to go to work. First thing in the morning, he planned to follow the visitors. He knew he was meant to work for their cause.

After the unification discussion, Bear Fat passed out gifts of jerked bear meat, rendered bear oil, and un-rendered bear fat. She also brought dried blueberries, plucked at the peak of ripeness on the side of the mountain. Every year upon her return, she generously shared those gifts with relatives, friends, and neighbors, a tradition which gave rise to her name, a name she had liked much better than her girlhood name, Too Skinny Girl. The gifts were well received. Most families had used up their reserves of bear fat. Some of the best uses for bear fat were softening the leathers and skins as part of the curing process, fortifying soups, and as a repellant to ward off the mosquitos and flies. Gentle Breeze liked to rub the fat between her toes to keep the dry skin on her feet from cracking.

After the council meeting, the village at Garoga Creek held a harvest celebration. The women had a great harvest in the fields and the men had successful hunts over the summer. There was plenty of bounty to share. All day long, women cooked their favorite meals, and about an hour before dark they brought their cook pots to the council commons at the center of the village. When everyone was full, the drumbeats began. Much of the village would celebrate deep into the night, dancing to the frenetic beat.

On the outer fringes of the council commons, Wanders Far sat, cross-legged, silently thinking about everything he had heard at the council meeting. His contemplative moment was to be short-lived.

When Somersault saw him from across the commons, she couldn't help herself. She let out a blood curdling scream, which most people would confuse for fear if they hadn't heard her before. As soon as the scream ended, her legs started moving. She flapped her arms and ran as fast as she could. When she reached Wanders Far, she jumped high in the air and landed smack on top of him, knocking him to the ground from his sitting position. Then she covered his cheeks with kisses. Very fast kisses, at least a hundred, while she laughed. Three-year-old Somersault was so happy to see Wanders Far, she couldn't control herself. It had been months since she had seen him last. Wanders Far couldn't help but laugh as well.

When she was done slobbering kisses all over his cheeks, she looked more closely. Something was different. This was not the uncle she knew. She screeched, "You have man hair now." Wanders Far was still lying on the ground, chuckling. The toddler pressed her forehead against Wanders Far's forehead, and her eyes were so close to Wanders Far's that when they blinked, their eyelashes touched. "Is that really you in there?"

Wanders Far tickled her mercilessly and she squealed with delight. Squash laughed at the sight. "Tonight, you can put her to bed, Brother!"

Wanders Far said, "I will, just as soon as I catch her."

Hearing that, Somersault took off, zigging and zagging throughout the village. Wanders Far reached into a bag he had strapped over his shoulder and asked Squash, "Can you look at this wampum belt and tell me its story when you get a chance?" Then he took off in hot pursuit of Somersault and patiently feigned a lack of ability to catch her. It took almost an hour for Somersault to tire, and then Wanders Far scooped her up and took her to the bunk in Squash's compartment in the longhouse. Wanders Far told Somersault a story about a family of magical, pink and purple skunks that smelled nice instead of stinky, and if they sprayed you, you would be super lucky instead of really sorry. He didn't have much of an ending planned for the story, but it didn't matter. She wouldn't be awake for the ending anyhow.

Squash was by the fire in the aisle in the middle of the longhouse, waiting for her younger brother. Wanders Far kneeled by the fire next to his sister. She was holding Follows Stars' belt. She spoke quietly, reverently even. "Wanders Far, this is the most amazing wampum belt I have ever seen. It looks to me like parts of it are very old." In the dim light provided by the fire, she showed him the symbols that told the stories of distant past generations of seers. Slowly she gave her interpretation of the stories, from left to right. About eight feet into the wampum belt, she got to the story of Follows Stars. She pointed to a symbol for a mountain, with a pond at the feet of it. Then a symbol of feet and a wavy line. "I think this symbol is meant to represent you, Wanders Far." Beneath that symbol was the symbol of a seer. "This tells me you are to be a runner and a seer, Brother. There are just a couple more symbols. I see a woman, a moon, a deer, the symbol for the color white, and the symbol for peace, larger than usually depicted, and the number five is overlaid with the peace symbol. Perhaps you can make sense of these symbols, Wanders Far. It looks like the last part of the belt was woven recently. It looks like the end of this is unfinished. I think someone has intended that more be added to this later." Squash looked up into her brother's eyes, just realizing the full impact of her reading, and more fully appreciating that her kid brother really had become a man. A man who would have an important destiny to fulfill.

"Would you keep that safe for me, Sister? It is too big to carry around, and too valuable to let anything happen to it." Wanders Far hugged Squash and told her how much he appreciated her help.

"I think I am going to need lots and lots of shells to tell your story, Brother," she concluded with a laugh. "You better make a long trip to the distant beaches or make great trades with our generous neighbors." Of course, the way she said *generous* was meant to be taken as sarcasm. Because of Bear Fat's position, the family trades were always most generous to the other side of such transactions.

Wanders Far told Squash that he would be on the trail the next day, and to tell Somersault he would bring her something.

The celebration continued in the commons but Wanders Far was ready to go to bed. He said goodbye to his sister and kissed his sleeping niece on the forehead. Then he made his way to his boyhood bunk at the other end of their longhouse. He wished that he could be there when Somersault woke up in the morning, and he knew she would be disappointed to find him gone.

Two hours before the sun came up, Wanders Far was on the trail, headed for the villages to the east. He was ready to fulfill his destiny, and he was excited to get started.

The morning after their homecoming celebration, Wanders Far

set out toward the east. He could have taken a canoe, and probably would have traveled faster, but he felt like following the trail along the river. He was a runner, and he wanted to be on foot. He managed to catch up with Two Rivers and Seeks Wampum just outside of the village at Cohoes Falls, fifty miles from the village at Garoga Creek.

Two Rivers and Seeks Wampum were standing at the foot of the falls, admiring the scenery. It was a gorgeous, enormous, thousand-foot wide crescent of water that spilled out over a dark-colored ledge of rocks, plunging into a pool 180 feet below. It was the most impressive waterfall along the People's River. Near the bottom of the falls was the village that Wanders Far had seen in his vision.

He introduced himself to the homely looking older man, and then to the handsome younger man. He told them that he had missed their visit at Garoga Creek. "I am a runner, and I would like to offer my services, carrying messages, and running ahead of your arrival in villages along your route. If I can be of use, and if you'll have me, it would be an honor to work with you," he offered humbly.

Two Rivers and Seeks Wampum looked at each other. They had been traveling with their message all summer, and so far, they had failed to convince anyone to fully buy into their plan. Sure, people had listened politely, and were willing to debate it. Then along came a young man offering to help. A young man who hadn't even heard their pitch. "We'd be glad to have you join us," said Seeks Wampum, who did most of the talking for the duo. Wanders Far followed the men into the village. They were trying to build a movement. They were desperate to generate a following, and they were glad to have a new disciple. Wanders Far was glad to find acceptance and relieved to know he had made it in time, just as he had foreseen. It was getting harder to deny the veracity of his visions.

They were politely received and were offered quarters in a longhouse that had some extra room. The council offered to hear their plan the next afternoon, which gave the two men a better opportunity to get to know the newest member of their troupe. Wanders Far told them the story of how he had won the round-trip race to the Great Roaring Waterfalls, far to the west, and then he told them about his annual trip to the giant mountains to the north. He did not share stories of his visions. He was sure that they would think he suffered from delusions if he had told them everything.

Seeks Wampum listened carefully to Wanders Far's stories, impressed with the teller, but not the telling. When Wanders Far finished, Seeks Wampum asked many questions. Then he asked, "Why don't you have a wampum belt to help you tell that story? A story like that is too good to be lost to history." Then he added in a friendly manner to soften the blow of criticism to come, "And a story that good shouldn't be told like that. Let me show you what I mean. Fetch our hosts!"

With the residents of the longhouse, including their host family assembled, Seeks Wampum stood in front of them with his feet spread wide apart, chest puffed out, and a twinkle in his eye. He retold the story he had just heard in an animated voice. His eyebrows seemed to jump all around his face and his fingers, hands, and arms moved fluidly and continuously. During the most exciting parts, he leaned forward. Sometimes he talked loud and fast, and sometimes he talked slowly and softly. The questions he had asked Wanders Far were worked into the retelling of the story. Wanders Far noticed that Seeks Wampum had added lots of colorful details, details that weren't true, but sure sounded entertaining. When the story was over, the tiny audience hooted, hollered, and congratulated Wanders Far. Then Seeks Wampum balled his fist and delivered a playful punch to Wanders Far's right shoulder. "That is how your story should be told, my friend."

Seeks Wampum basked in the glory of the audience's adoration. The host family included two young girls of marriageable age, and he had noticed them competing to try and catch his eye, and Seeks

Wampum seemed to encourage their attention. He was a good-looking man, single again at the age of 25, and his storytelling made him the center of attention wherever he went. He was well on his way to becoming a legendary ladies' man. He wasn't in a particular hurry to find a new wife yet. Traveling storytellers didn't make great husbands anyway.

After a few minutes of disorganized chatter, Seeks Wampum offered to tell another story. He took a wide belt out of his pack. Then he set a fat log upright and put his foot on it. He draped the wampum belt over his thigh and told the story of his friend and partner, Two Rivers, as slowly as possible, wringing every bit of drama from his terrible story, the symbols on the belt adding credibility to the telling.

Two Rivers was only 5-years-old when his entire family was brutally slain before his very eyes. His family lived in a village situated at the convergence of two large rivers of equal size. He was the first to be born at that village, so he was named for the location. His people were Cayuga, and his family had recently returned from a massive attack on an Oneida village. Their revenge was swift and disproportionate. The Cayuga had only killed one young brave, but it happened to be the son of a chief. Two Rivers' family had the misfortune of residing in the longhouse closest to the gates of their village, and their family also had the closest compartment to the entrance of their longhouse. One of the attackers was amused by the fight that the young boy had put up as the rest of his large family was swiftly slaughtered. The whole thing was over quickly, the attackers fleeing fast as the rest of the village began to respond. The young boy was thrown over the shoulders of the warrior he had tried to attack and taken back with the war party to the Oneida village, a gift for their chief, to replace his own lost son.

Seeks Wampum told the story of how Two Rivers grew up in his adopted family. For the first five years, he didn't talk at all. Then one day when he was 10-years-old, he ran around the village, screaming as if possessed. Everyone was shocked to see the quiet boy who slunk about the village suddenly seem to be possessed by a demon. His adopted family placed him in the charge of the seer. The seer was able to exorcise the boy's demons using hypnosis. While hypnotized, the boy talked normally, and the seer was convinced the boy had an extraordinary intellect. Unfortunately, when the boy was not under the spell of hypnosis, his brilliance was masked by a thick stutter. The boy never returned to the chief's family, and stayed with the seer, taking a keen interest in herbal remedies and philosophy.

Finally, Seeks Wampum told of having met Two Rivers in the woods one day the previous year. Two Rivers was gathering some wild mushrooms in the forest. It was nearing dark, so the two men decided to share a campsite. Having nothing better to do, Seeks Wampum patiently listened to Two Rivers talk about his idea of bringing together the people of the tribes who all shared the same language. "There are plenty of enemies to be found when our young warriors want to fight, but imagine how powerful a force we could be if we banded together, five tribes all in a line from east to west, the People of the Longhouses." Seeks Wampum was impressed by the brilliance of the plan. Considering Seeks Wampum wasn't interested in being a warrior, carrying Two Rivers' message of peace struck him as a good plan. Two Rivers sadly confided that he had been trying for many years to convince people to form a movement in favor of a unification plan.

After that night, the two traveled together, and gradually, the message that had been carried by Two Rivers was delivered by Seeks Wampum. Though they hadn't struck a quick following, the two agreed there was a sense of building acceptance. More people were listening, and people were listening longer. They were generating a reputation. Perhaps they needed to visit each village twice, or even more often than that, before it would become a movement.

With the storytelling ended, the host family went to bed. The three men talked about their plan for the next day. That's when the idea came to Two Rivers to try something drastic, and he suggested a dramatic, risky stunt. If he survived, it would seem that their cause had the Great Spirit's blessing. If he didn't survive, Seeks Wampum would be able to tell people about the man who believed in the plan so much, he was willing to give his life for the cause.

Wanders Far remained silent through the discussion about the plan. Seeks Wampum asked him what he thought of the idea. Wanders Far shrugged his shoulders and said, "I don't know, but I have a good feeling about it." He preferred not to share his vision with his friends. Better to let the vision play out however it was meant to. He still didn't see himself as a seer, but it was getting harder to deny when the visions seemed to unfold before his very eyes.

Seeks Wampum nodded proudly and said, "I just love to tell a story. Even better if I can be part of the story. Why, we'll all be heroes. Our people will benefit from this plan for years, maybe generations, and perhaps for eons. People will be telling stories and singing songs about us long after we're gone! What better way to protect our people and vanquish our enemies? Why, within twenty years, there won't be a Mohican, Huron, or Algonquin left alive!"

The plan they hatched the night before went off without a hitch. Wanders Far was impressed by how easily Two Rivers scampered to the top of the huge old Oak tree by the side of the river. Due to the size of the tree, it took quite some time to chop down. Seeks Wampum held the audience for over two hours, telling stories and making predictions, outlining a vision of peace and the prosperity the people would enjoy as a result. Seeks Wampum went on to predict the importance of the People of the Flint, who would become, notoriously, the People of the Eastern Gate.

Every detail Wanders Far had witnessed during his rite of passage materialized before his eyes. Unlike his new friend, Seeks

Wampum, Wanders Far had no great interest in becoming re-nowned. He couldn't fathom why the Great Spirit had chosen him as one to see visions, but was glad the Great Spirit had also chosen him to be a runner.

The next day, when the village awoke to find Two Rivers comfortably relaxing beside the campfire in the council commons area, the people from the village at Cohoes Falls were predictably convinced. One village didn't make a tribe, and one tribe didn't make a confederacy, but Two Rivers, Seeks Wampum, and Wanders Far were happy to have a commitment and were in great spirits as they began their way back along the path toward Wanders Far's village at Garoga Creek.

Seeks Wampum suggested that Wanders Far run ahead, tell the village that they were returning with big news, but not to disclose what it was. "See if you can create a sense of mystery and suspense, Wanders Far." Then Seeks Wampum asked if there was a weaver in his village who could capture the power of their new story in a wampum belt. Wanders Far told him about his sister, Squash. Seeks Wampum gave Wanders Far all the shells in his pack, a considerably large collection, and told Wanders Far the images that might be included in the belt. Wanders Far was back at Garoga Creek by midnight. Two Rivers and Seeks Wampum ambled into the village two evenings later.

Wanders Far introduced his new friends to his family and they made room for the visitors in Bear Fat's longhouse. Gentle Breeze gave up her compartment and bunked in her daughter's section of the longhouse, leaving the bunks in her compartment for Seeks Wampum and Two Rivers. The family gathered at the fire in the aisle between the compartments. Blue Arrow, Squash, and Somersault joined the small group. Somersault showed off a necklace, which Wanders Far made for her as he was walking back to the village. Squash presented the visitors with the belt she had made, working at top speed, recording the story that Wanders Far had told her.

Seeks Wampum was delighted and thanked Squash profusely. He told her honestly that he had never seen such beautiful work. "I must practice," he said, and the gathered family seemed pleased. With the new belt draped over his thigh, and his left foot on a stack of firewood, Seeks Wampum began. It was his first time retelling the story out loud, though he had practiced it in his mind on the fifty-mile hike between the villages. The symbols progressed perfectly along the belt, the story unfolding in chronological order. When he got to the symbol representing Wanders Far, he was surprised to also see the symbol of a seer. The audience noticed that the rhythmic cadence of Seeks Wampum's storytelling-spell had been broken. The teller was shocked to see the symbol of the seer. The family was also shocked to think of Wanders Far as a seer and everyone seemed to be looking back and forth between Wanders Far and Squash for an explanation. Slowly, Wanders Far shrugged his shoulders, his arms stretched out, as if to ask the Great Spirit, "Why is the symbol of the seer on the belt?" Squash copied the movement, mirroring Wanders Far, and helping to deflect from thoughts about Wanders Far being a seer. Seeks Wampum made direct eye contact with Wanders Far, and arched an eyebrow, seeming to say, "We will talk about this later, my friend." Then he resumed telling the story of how Two Rivers heroically demonstrated the Great Spirit's blessing for their unification plan.

Early the next morning, the three men met quietly to discuss the plan for addressing the council at Garoga Creek. Wanders Far knew it was coming. "Tell us about the seer's symbol," Two Rivers stuttered.

Wanders Far told them some more about his rite of passage and Follows Stars' role in presiding over it. He told them that he had foreseen the events at Cohoes Falls. He explained that he had had many visions through the years, but discounted them as dreams, fancies to occupy his mind while he burned the miles beneath his feet.

He told them he saw his role as a seer to be something he needed to develop and might one day be good at. The more Wanders Far tried to discount it and shrug it off, the more convinced Seeks Wampum and Two Rivers became. Wanders Far's skill as a seer could give their fledgling movement a powerful boost toward realization.

Before falling asleep in their bunks, Two Rivers confidentially whispered to Seeks Wampum, "How lucky to find this brilliant young man. Too bad he is so young and his talent is so raw. But he is just what our movement needs. I couldn't do this without you, Seeks Wampum, and we couldn't do this without our new friend either."

The presentation to the council at Garoga Creek went even better than the presentation at Cohoes Falls. What the latter had witnessed firsthand, the former had quickly converted to legend. It didn't hurt that the village at Garoga Falls was Wanders Far's home, and that his mother was the powerful, influential leader of the Women's Council.

The next day, several feet of snow interrupted their momentum. Two Rivers, Seeks Wampum, and Wanders Far spent the winter planning and strategizing. They agreed that it was time for the fledgling movement to become fully realized.

Chapter Nineteen
People of the Longhouse

A couple of months later it became clear that winter's grip had begun to lose hold, and warmer days began to melt the deep snow. It was still deep enough to require snowshoes, but the troupe couldn't wait any longer to get started. Two Rivers was thrilled to have Bear Fat and the entire Women's Council accompany them. First, they traveled a couple of miles to the northeast to the village where Fisher lived and convinced the Wolf Clan. Then they traveled ten miles to the southwest to Dandelion's village and persuaded the Turtle Clan village. The rest of their people's villages followed over the next several weeks.

They had won over one tribe, but to be considered a unification, they would need to convince a second tribe. Then they received tentative, measured support from the Oneida where Chipmunk lived. If others joined the confederacy, they would as well.

Wanders Far was sent ahead with messages for the Onondaga. The tour of the villages had lasted most of the spring, and by the time he reached the village on the banks of Cazenovia Lake, it was a week past the summer solstice. The weather was getting hotter. Summer had arrived.

Wanders Far continued to be nervous addressing councils and talking to powerful people he didn't know well. He took comfort and found confidence in his excellent memory and copied many of the words used by Seeks Wampum. Though he lacked the flair, his skills were quickly improving. He found himself increasingly comfortable saying the words he was meant to say. Wanders Far tended to prefer intimate settings, having one-on-one conversations or talking to small groups. He was happier on the outskirts and fringes of a celebration. His work as a runner often forced him to the center of the stage. It was meant to be. He must follow his path.

The chief of the Onondaga, a 40-year-old man named Entangled, was a powerful, ruthless, warlike ruler. He did what he pleased whenever he wanted, and he expected everyone else to do what *he* pleased, whenever *he* wanted, as well. He ascended to power solely because of his intimidating strength. The people were too afraid of him to stop him from demanding the title, essentially naming himself to the rank of chief.

Even after solidifying his power among his people, Entangled challenged the warriors of his own tribe, often beating them senseless, and several had been so thoroughly laid-out as to have lasting, permanent disabilities as a result. Finally, the women of the tribe appealed to his wife, Firefly, for mercy.

Entangled didn't care about many things and he certainly didn't care about his wife's thoughts or opinions, or any of the requests from the women of the village. More than anything else, he enjoyed battle, whether it was smashing his club into a human skull, plunging his knife into a person's body and splitting them open from end to end, or whether it was hand-to-hand combat, and it didn't matter much to him whether his victim was an enemy, or one of his own people. Entangled had a powerful ego and wanted to have the biggest tribe. He wanted everyone to know that his power could not be equaled and his achievements could not be bested. One day his wife suggested that their tribe might be bigger and stronger if he only battled the enemy, not his own people. He recognized that she had a point, and as a result, he spent most of his time outside the village in pursuit of enemies to vanquish near and far. That suited his wife just fine.

Entangled was a vile and disgusting man. He never bathed. He never tended to any sort of personal grooming, and he never allowed anyone else to assist with his grooming. His long dirty hair was matted and tangled, and in such a sorry state that children who looked at him thought that he had snakes attached to his scalp in place of his hair. Some of the adults even suspected it was true. Most of the people knew better than to look directly at their leader anyhow. If they had to be close to him at all, they generally tried to stay downwind.

Entangled was a member of the Oneida tribe before he married Firefly. He was a part of the small party that slaughtered the family of Two Rivers. Two Rivers never forgot the sound of Entangled's club crunching his mother's skull. Though it had happened twenty-five years earlier, it was still as vivid as the day she was killed.

Seeks Wampum grew up in a village near Wanders Far and had married a woman in Entangled's village six years earlier, at the age of 19. He had been the father of three young girls.

The first time Seeks Wampum and Two Rivers suggested a plan for peace among the tribes, Entangled retaliated against what he perceived to be a challenge to his authority by stomping into Seeks Wampum's longhouse, grabbing his oldest daughter by the ankles, taking her outside, and swinging her tiny body upside down into the nearest tree. Her brain exploded upon impact, and her tiny lifeless body fell to the ground. As quick as he had arrived, he stomped away and was gone.

Even after the devastating loss, Seeks Wampum and Two Rivers persisted in their valiant unification effort. They tried to go behind Entangled's back, making their case to tribal elders. One day, Entangled got wind of their plotting. When Seeks Wampum returned to his home, he found that the rest of his family had been slain.

Seeks Wampum's wife had begged him to give up and she had begged him to stay away from Two Rivers. She had agreed that it was a noble cause, but not so noble a cause that she should have her baby girl gruesomely murdered before her eyes. Seeks Wampum tried to make his wife understand. Perhaps hundreds, or even thousands of their people could be saved, if they could just find a way to get their chief to understand that their plan was also good for him. He never imagined his entire family brutally murdered by their own leader. He could hear her pleading voice begging him to drop the issue, every time he thought of her, yet their deaths seemed to make him even more committed to the cause.

Seeks Wampum's story weighed heavy in Wanders Far's mind on his way to the Onondaga village. He knew the message he carried was the same message that got Seeks Wampum's family killed. It was too threatening to the status quo.

While waiting to address the counsel, Wanders Far sat observing Entangled. He surveyed the man's soul. His reputation preceded him. Wanders Far had heard many stories about the brutality of the man, above and beyond what he had done to the families of Seeks Wampum and Two Rivers. Wanders Far's assessment was that there was a fire in Entangled' soul and a pitch-black darkness at the same time. He was always wary of speaking at council meetings, even without the presence of Entangled. The importance of the issue to his people's future also added to Wanders Far's worries. He was not an impartial messenger. He was part of the unification movement. He knew he had to contain his enthusiasm.

Wanders Far shared information as a runner, just the facts, and not as a participant in the movement. He had been well-warned by his friends. He concluded his short remarks by suggesting the most powerful leader of the most powerful village could be the leader of the entire confederacy. They could increase their power, and they would be more feared by their enemies, especially the Hurons and Algonquins, if they banded together. The carefully crafted message succeeded and Entangled was intrigued. Wanders Far relayed an invitation for Entangled to meet at the location that was known as the "Road to War" the next evening.

At the intersection of two major trails, one going north and south and the other going east to west was a large longhouse occupied by a handsome looking, single, 30-year-old woman. It was rare for anyone to live outside the protection of a village, fortified by palisade walls, no less an unmarried woman. Inside there was just one compartment at the far end. The rest of the longhouse was completely open space, with a large fire at the middle. There was enough space to seat a large war party or a group of hunters.

Miraculously, the woman who lived there managed to maintain complete impartiality, affiliation with no tribe, and not seeming to prefer one tribe to another, so all tribes protected her. Her home was a safe haven. She was named after the location, Road to War, with the long form of her name being She Who Lives Along the Road to War. Warriors and hunters brought her gifts, and in return found a warm fire and usually a fine meal as well.

Entangled arrived on time and found himself alone with Road to War. Entangled was a frequent visitor. It was a perfect location for the warlike leader. He seemed to enjoy and appreciate the presence and convenience of the home belonging to Road to War. It was a place for him to brag and be admired. Entangled dreamed of being worshipped by his people and feared by his enemies. Road to War's home was the perfect setting for Entangled's reputation to be touted. Thus far, Entangled had honored the sanctity of the safe haven.

A few days earlier, the friends had won their hostess over to the notion of uniting the tribes. Although she had maintained impartiality with respect to matters of war, she was in fact rather partial to peace. Road to War readily volunteered to secure Entangled's commitment to the plan. Though Two Rivers and Seeks Wampum had preferred a plan that involved death by toxic substances, Road to War was unwilling to be involved in a *lethal* poisoning.

Entangled arrived right on time and she was ready. She had prepared a hearty meal. It was enough for an entire war party, rather than a dinner for two. Entangled over-indulged. Road to War skipped the stew. After dinner, she prepared a pipe for him. Whether it was because of the mushrooms in the stew, the hard cider, or the aromatics in the pipe, Entangled was in no mood to argue when she suggested a warm bath, which she just happened to have prepared. She suggested that a powerful leader should look his best. Though he didn't care about hygiene, it didn't occur to him to object. She scrubbed his back and began to give voice to a vision of the united people and went to great lengths to describe a man so powerful that he could unite them all. A man who could serve as the chief of the confederacy. Why not the most powerful leader, from the most powerful village, who just so happened to be a member of the middle of the five tribes. Not only would he be the most powerful ruler of their time, but as their very first united chief, his status would be that of the most legendary leader of all time.

When his bath was over, he almost looked presentable for the first time in twenty years. As soon as the bath was over, she wrapped him in a warm robe and he passed out. He slept solidly for the next twelve hours. Road to War watched over him and imagined his doting mother watching over his sleeping body forty years earlier. She shuddered to think that Entangled could ever have been lovable.

In the morning, she was ready with a hearty breakfast. The moment he awoke, Road to War continued her appeal to Entangled's ego, and suggested that runners be sent immediately to bring leaders representing the villages from all five tribes to meet at his village. Only he was powerful enough to make this happen. In case he might have forgotten the arguments she made the night before, she repeated the highlights quickly over breakfast. Entangled was in no mood to question or argue. He felt miserable and he had no idea why.

Shortly after breakfast, Two Rivers and Seeks Wampum arrived, and half an hour later, Wanders Far and several runners from Entangled's village appeared. Everyone addressed Entangled as if he were already the leader of all of the tribes, just as they had conspired to do. Within an hour, all were dispatched to invite leaders from all the villages of all five tribes to attend a council at Cazenovia Lake twenty days following. Entangled made plans for a quick military campaign to the north and asked Road to War if she would travel to his village and make the arrangements for the many visitors that would be coming.

The village at Cazenovia Lake was the largest village Wanders Far had ever seen, encircled by three rings of palisade fencing rather than two. It was home to over a hundred longhouses, and home as well to the powerful warlike chieftain.

After the council meeting was over, there was a feast. It was a massive celebration. The guests and the hosts celebrated the commitment of four of the five tribes. The Seneca, to the far west, remained unconvinced.

When the feast concluded, well after dark, most of the younger children were put to bed. Older children, young adults, and adults of all ages enjoyed a long, festive evening around the bonfire, and dancing to the rhythm of the rattles and drums.

Wanders Far was gathered near a large group of people about his own age. Though he preferred to remain at the outer perimeter, quietly enjoying being part of the special celebration commemorating the epic unification, it was not to be. Question after question brought Wanders Far to the center of the gathering and Wanders Far told them about some of the amazing things he had seen in his travels.

A young girl named Bright Star caught the eye of Wanders Far. As Wanders Far answered questions and told stories, he focused his answers directly at her. He could barely take his eyes off her. Of course, everyone noticed. Certainly, Bright Star noticed.

Wanders Far told about his summer trips to the mountains, and his climb up the highest mountain he had ever seen, and then he told them about seeing the snow-white deer on the way up.

Bright Star interrupted, laughed, and proclaimed that if he could bring her the skin of that deer for her wedding dress, she would have no choice but to marry *him*. Wanders Far's heart raced at the thought, then he was brought back to earth as a young man called Snapping Turtle shared with Wanders Far that Bright Star had no fewer than five other men attempting to perform some impossible feat to win the heart of Bright Star. He joked, "You had better hurry!" Then Snapping Turtle laughed and said that Bright Star probably would never find a husband with such unrealistic expectations.

The next day, Two Rivers, Seeks Wampum, Wanders Far, and several tribal elders left Cazenovia Lake to attend a council for the Seneca—at Canandaigua Lake. That lake was known to them as the *chosen spot*.

Summer was half over. The three friends gathered to discuss their plan for the next day. Though they had dared to dream they could bring the five nations together, they had to admit that they surprised themselves at how quickly it seemed to be happening. Before Wanders Far joined Two Rivers and Seeks Wampum, they had only realized limited success. Seeks Wampum smiled broadly in the light of the small campfire on the edge of the big lake and told Wanders Far that he was their good luck charm. "You have magic in your soul, friend."

Wanders Far bowed his head slightly, and accepted the compliment. As Two Rivers suggested different approaches they could take at council the following day, Wanders Far doodled in the dirt with a long poker-stick. In the middle of the design was a simple symbol for a pine tree, a basic triangle with a small rectangular trunk at the bottom. Two squares to the left, and two squares to the right, and lines connecting each symbol to the next. The five symbols represented the tribes and their alliance. Wanders Far had drawn it absentmindedly.

Seeks Wampum began jumping up and down and flapping his arms, loudly interrupting Two Rivers. "What have you done. What have you drawn! Wow. That's just what we need. You have captured the power. Imagine how that will look on a wampum belt." With that, Seeks Wampum was gone, with no explanation to his friends. He had met a young woman in the village earlier that afternoon who liked to weave. Seeks Wampum begged her family to let the young woman work through the night. He stayed by her side all night long, and by morning, it was done except for the last symbol, the one representing the People of the Flint. It was a good thing that the council meeting wasn't due to begin until midday. Seeks Wampum dozed for two hours while the young woman finished the belt.

The Seneca elders seemed to enjoy sitting on the fence. Perhaps they hoped to gain some gifts or some kind of special advantage by holding out. The discussion went around and around, and around again, everyone giving voice to one point of view or another. Advantages and disadvantages were listed and measured against one another. Nobody seemed to be in any hurry to conclude the discussion until some of the elders began discussing another important issue, preparations for an assault on their Erie enemies to the southwest. Seeks Wampum had been holding the belt, to be used if needed to clinch the deal, or if the deal had been easily done to celebrate the deal. He was just about to pull the belt from his pack when everyone began to look toward the sky.

It had been a perfectly clear day, not a cloud in the sky. Suddenly, it was getting dark. The moon was beginning to blot out the sun.

Wanders Far screamed, "Don't look at it. It will blind you. Look at the reflection of it in the lake." He screamed so loudly and unexpectedly, he surprised himself. He had no idea why he said what he did, but everyone obeyed. They stood in total silence in the dark in the middle of the afternoon, until finally the moon began to move away. The assembled crowd sighed with relief.

"It's a miracle! The Great Spirit has spoken," Seeks Wampum shouted. "Look!" He held the belt, draped over his wrists. In addition to the symbol Seeks Wampum had asked the young woman to put on the belt, she had also added a symbol for the sun and a symbol for the moon. She had no idea why she did it, except that Seeks Wampum had fallen asleep. Rather than wake him, she just wove the extra symbols and couldn't explain why she felt compelled to do it.

Naysayers were powerless to argue further. Tribal elders looked at one another in disbelief. The decision had made itself. Unification was complete and ratified. The five tribes were a confederacy.

After the council, the three friends congratulated each other mightily. After a few minutes of jovial back-slapping and celebrating, Wanders Far abruptly proclaimed, "I must go. I have things I need to do at once. I will miss you, friends." Before they could comprehend that he was leaving, he was gone.

Chapter Twenty
The Great White Stag

The equinox was maybe a month away. Snapping Turtle's words rattled around in Wanders Far's head. *No fewer than five other men attempting to perform some impossible feat to win the heart of Bright Star. You had better hurry!*

It was a very late start. By that time of year, his family would be getting ready to return home from the mountains. He was only just setting out, and he was hundreds of miles to the west of their usual starting point.

He felt some sadness about leaving the lake. Looking back at it from a small hill, it looked like a long bean in the distance. He marched on. There were many miles of daylight remaining, and perhaps he might walk through the night. As he walked he thought about the events of the previous several days, his great friends and their big dream, and the dramatic movement of the moon and the sun. Then he thought of his vision on the top of the mountain, the vision of his "Moon Girl." In the days that followed his departure from Canandaigua Lake, he felt invincible. Yet there was much to do. Wanders Far walked with the sense of purpose that comes from the feeling that he was following his destiny. He had 280 miles to hike and a stag to slay.

When he arrived at Garoga Creek for rest and provisions, he was surprised to see his mother and father had remained in the village during the summer. His father had broken his leg. There was no bear harvest. Wanders Far felt guilty thinking that his family had needed him while he was away. "I'll bring back bear while I'm away! I promise," he said, and the next morning he was off again.

He knew the way by heart, having followed the route every summer he could remember. If it were possible, he was even more excited than he had been before. There was something about making the quest on his own and there was also something about the importance of that trip to his family and the village, let alone his own future and he was powered by purpose. If he succeeded, he would marry that Moon Girl—the girl of his dreams. He would join her people at Cazenovia Lake. He fantasized about bringing his young wife to the mountains and watching the sun set with her on the top of the great mountain. What a great wedding trip that would be. And Wanders Far thought about raising their children and the trips they would make to Copperas Pond every summer.

Merely ten days after leaving the shores of Canandaigua Lake, Wanders Far was standing alone on the edge of Copperas Pond. He sparked a small fire in the pit outside the wickiup. Usually Wanders Far relished solitary moments, but that was a place that was supposed to be filled with the happy sounds of his family enjoying the best days of their year. He stayed one night and decided to move his base camp to the little mountain. He felt the spirit of his friend Follows Stars calling him there. Wanders Far thought that on one hand it was hard to believe Follows Stars had been gone a year, and on the other hand so much had happened since the previous summer, it was hard to comprehend that it had *only* been a year. However long, Wanders Far enjoyed having Follows Stars' spirit active in his heart as he set out to complete his work on the mountain.

Wanders Far spent every waking hour of the following week in pursuit of the great white stag. One day he whispered into a breeze,

"If this is my destiny, why am I having to work so hard to achieve it," as if he had a right to question the Great Spirit. In that week he had caught glimpses, but the agile, athletic deer safely remained a sufficient distance from the tips of Wanders Far's arrows. Fortunately, a deer wasn't known to venture more than a mile from its territory, as long as it found everything it needed there.

The season was late. He was frustrated. Wanders Far decided to take a couple of days away from the hunt. From previous experience he knew that taking a few steps away from the task at hand often helped him get closer to his objective in the long run. At first he felt foolish, wasting time to go exploring. An hour down the trail he felt more like himself. Perhaps he could afford a few days away from his quest.

He came off the mountain on the back side, near a waterfall, and continued along until he found Silver Lake. He spent a day on the banks of the lake and saw an island. He swam to the island, not far from the shore. It was nearing dark. He made a fire, and at dusk, he noticed another string of smoke in the evening sky. He was not alone on the island.

He quietly set out to investigate. An ancient Algonquin was sitting by the campfire, making arrows. When Wanders Far realized he was Algonquin, he started to back away, thinking he was undetected. The Algonquin heard him, and said, "I hear you. I see you. Sit by my fire in friendship, Son." He was old enough to feel comfortable calling any man *son*.

Wanders Far came in to the old man's camp. He hadn't seen a human being in weeks.

"Do you remember me, Son?" the old man asked.

Wanders Far thought about it. He didn't need to concentrate so hard. His young memory was usually very reliable.

"You know me as Blue Arrow's grandfather," the old man added.

"It's great to see you, Grandfather." Wanders Far recalled his friend and traveling to Cave Eye village. Wanders Far recalled seeing Blue Arrow's grandfather hunched over a fire, wearing a blanket over his head, and sitting in a dark doorway. He couldn't recall ever having gotten a good look at the old man. It was no wonder he didn't recall having met him.

"You can call me Blue Ears. I am a seer. I feel the presence of an old friend. Do you have news of He Who Follows the Stars?"

Wanders Far answered slowly, "Yes, Grandfather. He Who Follows the Stars guided me through my rites of passage last summer, and then he joined the Great Spirit. I am so sorry to have to tell you about the loss of your friend."

"A double passage! What power," Blue Ears proclaimed. Then he continued, "I make magic arrows that are truer than the hunters' aim. The arrows I make fly where the hunter wants them to go, not where he aims them. The bows I make send arrows farther, and faster, and are one hundred times more powerful than other arrows. I think that is why you are here, Wanders Far," he said the young man's name so slowly, it was as if he were making a long voyage. "You must promise this bow and these magic arrows will never be used in battle. If one of my Algonquin tribesmen is brought down by this bow, you too will be brought down."

Wanders Far had no gift to share in return, aside from the nearly empty parfleche he carried at his side. The Algonquin considered the bow and arrows more of a gift than a trade but accepted the reciprocal gift nonetheless.

Two days later, Wanders Far was back on the little mountain with his new bow and magic arrows. And perhaps the magic laws of attraction drew the great white stag to Wanders Far. Slowly, majestically, prince-like, the stag ascended the mountain. Near the top, the regal deer stopped and stood on a rocky precipice, bathed in a beam of glorious sunlight through a small hole in an otherwise cloudy sky. Wanders Far was some distance below. He notched two arrows in the bow at one time, like the old Algonquin had instructed him to do. He aimed just higher than his target and he pulled the bow back as far as he could and let the arrows loose. The sound of the arrows leaving the bow was indeed much louder than Wanders Far was accustomed to hearing. The arrows sped quickly and surely to their target, and magically they were strong enough to lift the massive stag in the air and pin him to the rocks on the mountain, twenty feet from the precipice Wanders Far stood on. Impossibly, the deer was a hundred feet above any point to which Wanders Far could reach or climb, one arrow through the neck, and another through the haunch. Wanders Far had never seen an arrowhead powerful enough to penetrate into solid rock. The magic of Blue Ears' arrows defied explanation.

All afternoon Wanders Far tried to find a way to free the noble stag from the rocks, to no avail. He stood on the precipice where the deer had stood and tossed large pine branches. He tried to throw rocks and managed to hit the arrows a couple of times, but still, no luck. Finally, he made camp near the summit of the little mountain and looked up at the peak above. First, he gathered large, dry branches of deadfall, then he climbed to the summit of the giant mountain. From there he hiked-back down to just above where the deer hung, and tried to drop heavy branches to loosen the arrows' hold on the rocks.

Then he began work on a long ladder. He chose two long, thin pine trees, chopped them down, and removed all the branches. He worked until midnight, attaching rungs using every inch of the strong twine he had at his disposal. It would be a perilous climb up the rickety ladder. He hoped it would hold him.

When he returned with the heavy ladder first thing in the morning for a fresh look at the problem, he found that the body of the stag was missing. The two arrows remained in the rock. There was no other sign of the stag having existed except for the arrows. Wanders

Far stood for a full ten minutes, puzzled. Then he noticed the gray rock had all turned to white. Awestruck, Wanders Far was certain that it was a sign from the Great Spirit. What could the sign mean? He must find someone to interpret the message. Blue Ears!

Wanders Far returned to the little island near the banks of Silver Lake. The old Algonquin was still there, seeming not to have moved an inch in the days since Wanders Far last saw him. He listened to Wanders Far's retelling of the hunt for the great white stag. Then the Algonquin laughed mightily. He claimed the magic of the arrows came from spirits in the sky. Then he concluded, "Yes, friend. The Great Spirit has wonderful plans for you. Hold your head high. Realize your dreams. You must also prepare for some surprises. That is all I can tell you!"

Wanders Far camped with the Algonquin that night. They had a good time telling stories and shared a nice meal. In the morning, Wanders Far left the island with almost more arrows than he could carry.

He dedicated the next couple of weeks to hunting bears. He returned to the ridge his father had shown him. He filled the bait box with fish and waited. An hour later, the largest bear he had ever seen approached the bait. With the aid of the magic arrows and a high perch above, Wanders Far brought down the colossal beast with one arrow. He processed the bear at his camp on the mountain. Wanders Far also followed his father's trail to several other bait stops. Within a week he had also shot a medium bear and a smaller bear. He thought of bringing the small bearskin home as a gift for his favorite niece.

It took Wanders Far several days to finish processing the bears. The nights grew dramatically colder and the fall colors were spectacular. Usually the family returned from the mountains long before the trees dropped their leaves. Wanders Far felt lucky to be witnessing the glorious sight, and yet he worried that winter might come too soon. Finally, his work was done. He used the remains of the ladder he constructed to fashion another travois. He tied the meat, fat, and skins to the travois and set off down the mountain.

Before returning home, Wanders Far spent a second night at Copperas Pond. He couldn't explain what possessed him to sweep the floor and clean the small longhouse there, except that he must be doing it for his mother's benefit. That was the first summer his mother and father had not made the trip to Copperas Pond. A tear sprang from the corner of his eye and darted over the edge of his cheekbone. As the sun began to set, Wanders Far climbed up to the ledge. Frivolously, he hollered, "Who says a man can't act like a child now and then." Then he jumped off the rock. He recalled the time his grandmother jumped off the rock into the pond. Wanders Far suddenly felt alone. Lonely even. Usually one to seek the solitude of time alone, he suddenly began to yearn for his family back on the banks of Garoga Creek, and of course he yearned to see Bright Star. He had a couple of deerskins for her, and the Great Sprit's blessing. He couldn't wait to get home, and beyond that he couldn't wait to get back to the Onondaga camp, eighty miles beyond. Surely Bright Star would hear of the Great Spirit's blessing and joyfully settle for an average, fawn-colored ceremonial wedding dress. Before leaving camp, Wanders Far wrapped the magic bow and arrows in an old skin. He placed it in a hole on a dry hillside between two large boulders and covered the base of the boulders with smaller rocks. Then he brushed the surroundings with a large pine bough to make the area look like it had always been that way. With his pack overflowing and his travois sticks at his hips, he made the slow walk to water and the series of walks, paddles, and portages that would lead him home and into the promising future his seer guides told him about.

His family was mighty glad to see him, and the provisions he brought were warmly received. That night they listened in amazement as he told them the story of the great white stag. The skin of the mighty bear was compared in size to all the other bearskins in the longhouse. Big Canoe brought out the largest skin he had, and it was smaller. Big Canoe beamed with pride at his son's trophy.

Chapter Twenty-One
Justice

The next morning, Wanders Far set out for Bright Star's camp, full of hope, excitement, and pride. It took several days to reach the Onondaga village. He had been away for a while, and a lot had changed. After sharing the news from his tribe and from the villages in between, Wanders Far's heart fell from his chest upon seeing Bright Star, hand in hand with her new husband. The young man who had chided that Bright Star would never find a husband because of her overly challenging missions had somehow sufficiently impressed her and convinced Bright Star's family to let him marry her. Wanders Far's head dropped, and his shoulders sank. He felt wounded, angry, and betrayed.

He mumbled some nice things he didn't mean to the happy young couple and abruptly turned to go. He had a sick feeling in the pit of his stomach. His cheeks felt hot. He wanted to escape as fast as he could. In his haste, Wanders Far ran smack into the most beautiful girl he had ever seen, and both of them tumbled to the ground. Strangely, she looked like Bright Star. They could have been identical twins.

He jumped to his feet, apologizing profusely, then reached down and took her hands in his. She was a little disoriented. Wanders Far helped her to her feet. She stood in front of him, her hands in his, gripping tight so he wouldn't let go. She said, "I am Trillium, Bright Star's sister."

Trillium's heart raced. She had noticed Wanders Far on his previous visit. She knew that he was competing for a chance to marry her sister. Every night she wished that her sister would marry someone else and then she wished that Wanders Far would marry her instead. Trillium was delighted when Bright Star married Snapping Turtle and had been impatiently waiting for Wanders Far to return ever since. It had only been a couple of weeks since Bright Star's wedding, but to Trillium it seemed like months. She confided in her best friend and cousin, an older girl named Justice, who lived in the next compartment of her longhouse. Justice helped Trillium concoct a plan to be tripped over, then Justice helped Trillium enact the plan. At just the right moment, Justice practically tossed Trillium to the ground at Wanders Far's feet. Her timing was perfect.

Trillium felt awkward, standing there in front of Wanders Far, holding his hands so tightly. She knew she should let go but instead she tightened her grip further. She had his attention. He was looking directly down into her eyes. She felt like he was looking down into her soul, like he knew exactly what she was thinking. Maybe he was just being nice. Maybe he was suffering from a loss of words. Maybe he was figuring out how to get his hands back so he could leave. Though she was filled with doubt, she held on firmly nonetheless.

Wanders Far stood before Trillium. Looking into her eyes, he saw their future. He knew her heart. He realized that he had never known Bright Star's heart. His photographic memory replayed his vision of Moon Girl. He felt his heart thumping in his chest. After all that longing for Bright Star, and all that effort in pursuit of the great white stag, he stood there realizing that he had mistakenly overlooked Trillium, the real Moon Girl. He felt foolish, having pursued Bright Star, having never held her hands, having never spent any time with her. He already felt a deep connection with Trillium, though he had not yet said a single word to her. Then he felt a blast of adrenaline shoot through his gut. He was standing there like an idiot. She expected him to say something. He wondered how long he had been standing there. He thought frantically about what he should say. Thankfully, the words came. "Can I walk you home, Trillium?"

Trillium was relieved. He had spoken. He had said her name. She couldn't recall having heard anything sound as good as the way his voice sounded when he said her name. Then she thought about what else he said. "No," she said almost too sharply. Then she suggested, "Let's go for a walk along the lake, instead." Trillium finally released her hold on Wanders Far's hands. Quickly, Trillium turned to her cousin and asked if she would let her mother know that she would be home later. Justice had no opportunity to decline.

Trillium quickly took Wanders Far's hand again, and they left the village through the opening in the palisade walls. They walked a short distance to the shore of the lake. Across the lake and above the trees the sun was slowly reaching the horizon, radiating bright warm colors, red, orange, yellow, and pink. They stood side by side, hand in hand, and watched the sun prepare to set for a couple of minutes. Then Trillium stood before Wanders Far, on the tips of her toes, both of her hands in his, and she kissed him, ever so gently, and ever so briefly on his lips. Then they held each other's gaze for several seconds.

As he looked into her eyes, Wanders Far noticed that her head was completely framed by the circle of the setting sun, and he was taken back to his vision. He closed his eyes, and then he kissed her, briefly, but a little longer than before. They looked into each other's eyes again, answering each other's questions without speaking.

Wanders Far kissed her again, released her hands, and they embraced. With one hand on her shoulder, and another at the small of her back, he pulled her tightly to him. Trillium wrapped her arms around his back. An hour later they were startled by Justice, who had been sent to find Trillium. Trillium gave Wanders Far a quick, sweet, parting kiss and dutifully followed her cousin back to the village.

Wanders Far watched until they disappeared through the entrance. Then he sat by the side of the lake, legs stretched out before him, toes pointing due west. There was no moon in the sky, but the stars seemed to twinkle brighter than usual against a dark blue background. He had fallen completely in love. He felt good, yet he ached to be separated from her, even until the next day. Wanders Far thought Trillium was prettier than Bright Star, not to mention having a far sweeter demeanor, and then on top of that, Trillium didn't expect Wanders Far to travel hundreds of miles in pursuit of a gift to win her heart. Instead of returning to the home of his host in the village, Wanders Far slept under the stars by the lake.

In the morning, Trillium and Justice arrived at the lake with fifteen small children of various ages. Most days they watched over whatever children needed watching while their mothers attended to other work. The girls were responsible for the safety of the children. They enjoyed spending their time teaching and playing with the children, and they enjoyed working together. A year earlier, Justice had received a new name due to her ability to solve squabbles, smooth over hurt feelings, and soothe wounded egos following fights between and among the children that occurred from time to time. Wanders Far watched as Trillium settled a batch of giggling toddlers in a ring, tickling them and making faces. It wasn't long before Wanders Far had been called to entertain as well, on hands and knees giving the older children rides around on the grass.

Entangled and a dozen warriors passed by, sneered to see a full-grown man playing with children, and barked an order. Wanders Far stood obediently. He stood, stiff and rigid in the direct presence of the chief, wondering if he should say anything or just stand there.

It occurred to the chief that it had been a long time since he had

had the pleasure of smashing his fist into anybody. There must be an enemy to vanquish. He heard Road to War's voice in his head warning him against being harsh with his own people. He couldn't stop himself. With all the force in his muscular body, he whacked Wanders Far with an open hand. Wanders Far was sent flying back into the dirt, landing ten feet away from Entangled, who was already on the move. His back was turned and his feet were on the path with his warriors before Wanders Far even realized what had happened to him.

Wanders Far was more surprised than hurt. Trillium rushed to his side. Wanders Far stood proudly, spat into the wind, puffed his chest out, and crossed his arms. *Our people should not follow that man*, Wanders Far thought. He dared not say it out loud.

The children froze and sat quietly until Entangled and his men were completely out of sight.

That evening, Wanders Far was invited to dinner at Trillium's longhouse. It only had six compartments. Trillium was the youngest of six children, and her father had been killed in one of Entangled's battles ten years earlier. Her brothers had married and moved to other villages. Trillium and her mother lived in one compartment. Bright Star and Snapping Turtle lived in a second compartment. Justice and her mother lived in a third compartment. Following the unification, Road to War moved to the Onondaga village, leaving her solitary home at the junction of the paths, and she occupied a fourth compartment. The fifth and sixth compartments weren't yet occupied.

After dinner, they talked about life in their village, which essentially served as the capital of the confederacy of the tribes. Entangled, in his quest for military victories, left it to Road to War to administer the village itself. His only interest in governance was to increase the size and value of his empire. Road to War explained to Wanders Far that she based her leadership of the village on the model she had heard from him about Bear Fat's matriarchy at Garoga Creek. With

Seeks Wampum at her side telling powerful stories, Road to War implemented the same model at the Onondaga village. Gradually, the other tribes, clans, and villages had begun to implement the same model throughout the confederacy. She told Wanders Far that the village had changed her name to New Face.

Then Wanders Far was called upon to tell his life's story, and the story of all the members of his family. By the time he was finished it was late in the evening. Everyone headed to their bunks. Trillium left with Wanders Far, and they shared a long, passionate embrace in the shadows of a dark, cloudy night. Between the children at the lake and the family at dinner, they hadn't had any time alone together that day. Again, their parting was hastened by Justice interrupting, "Come along, Trillium. It's time to say goodnight!"

The following morning, Trillium found Wanders Far sitting at the side of the lake. Clouds were swirling in the sky. It was colder than the preceding days. The season was changing. She sat next to him.

Sadly, Wanders Far said, "It will snow soon. Winter is coming. I have messages I have to deliver. Soon the people will be stuck in their villages for the winter." Wanders Far looked at Trillium and she understood what he was saying. It was time for Wanders Far to leave. His pack was ready at his side.

They stood up, and he wrapped her in his arms. He looked seriously into her eyes. He confessed to being completely and hopelessly in love with her. She kissed him warmly. Then he continued, "Winter will separate us. In the spring, I will ask my mother to negotiate a marriage for us, if you'll have me."

Trillium answered silently, with another warm, passionate kiss. Then she said, "Yes, of course I'll have you." Tears streamed down her face. It was a brief, yet powerful courtship, and it would be followed by a long separation. "I will long for you while we are apart. This will be the longest winter of my life, Wanders Far."

They consoled each other for a few more minutes. Then Wanders Far whispered, "I must go now, Trillium." She watched him depart, and he turned to look back at her three times before he disappeared into the forest. She stood there, missing him already, thinking about how less than a week earlier she had jealously hoped to win the affections of her sister's former suitor. Then just several days later, the love of her life was on his way to arrange for their marriage. She sighed deeply, the sort of sigh that predicted a long winter of waiting.

On the long trek back to his mother's longhouse, Wanders Far thought about what Blue Ears, the old Algonquin seer, had told him. "The Great Spirit has wonderful plans for you. Hold your head high. Realize your dreams. But prepare for some surprises." His mentor, Follows Stars, had cautioned him, warning, "Just because you see a little, doesn't mean you know the whole thing."

Miles of walking along the trails toward home gave Wanders Far lots of time to think about his past and his future. He had thought Bright Star was the love of his life. He hadn't even noticed her younger sister on his previous trips.

The first day of his journey was a gray, cloudy day, and it grew colder as the day went by. The second day was colder than the first, and a light snow began to fall shortly after sunrise. It crossed his mind that he was glad to have the physical challenge of the weather. Somehow that seemed to assuage the loneliness of his separation from Trillium. The third day was colder yet. The snow had stopped, after leaving the season's first snowfall of about 8 inches. Fortunately Wanders Far knew the trail without having to see where it was. He plodded on and reached his village at the end of the third day.

Bear Fat was happy to see Wanders Far when he arrived at Garoga Creek just before dinner. He hadn't been gone very long. She wondered whether he had good news, or disappointing news, having been aware that he was on his way to ask an Onondaga girl to marry him. He wasn't saying anything, and she couldn't tell by looking at him. The suspense was gnawing on her all through dinner. She could hardly wait until they finished eating. Gentle Breeze unsuccessfully encouraged Wanders Far to eat more.

They were about to settle around the hearth when Somersault came running through the longhouse, jumped into the air, and was scooped up by Wanders Far. She had a hundred questions, which Wanders Far answered happily. Bear Fat waited impatiently. Unfortunately, Somersault didn't ask the question Bear Fat was hoping to have answered.

Finally, they sat cross-legged around the fire. It was past Somersault's bedtime. She made herself at home on Wanders Far's lap, listened for a little while, then fell sound asleep. Wanders Far told a very detailed story about his trip to the Onondaga village. Then he told his family about Bright Star and Snapping Turtle. He made it a point to look sad, then he tipped his head back up, cocked it slightly sideways, raised an eyebrow, and told his family about crashing into Trillium. He raced through the rest of the story to get to the part where he told them that he had asked Trillium to marry him. Bear Fat beamed when she heard the end of the story. She clasped her hands together beneath her chin. She couldn't wait to make the trip.

All winter she hoarded anything she thought could be used in the marriage negotiations. The trip to Copperas Pond would have to wait until Bear Fat and her family made a long trip to the Onondaga village. She was looking forward to visiting the new capital of their confederacy. Wanders Far went on to tell the story of New Face. It pleased Bear Fat to hear Wanders Far explain how New Face styled the Onondaga village after Bear Fat's leadership.

The following morning, Somersault was surprised to hear that Wanders Far was going to marry a flower. She didn't understand. Trillium was named after a delicate, three petaled, wild woodland flower that bloomed in the spring.

Winter held its grip longer than usual. It was a long, cold season.

It was the kind of winter that left supplies dangerously low, and the people would have to work hard to replenish their food storage. That spring they dug into the emergency corn cache they had buried outside the village.

The snow hadn't finished melting. Both Wanders Far and Bear Fat had been trying to melt the snow with their thoughts. Finally, they had waited long enough. Bear Fat, Big Canoe, and Wanders Far set off down the trail to the west. Wanders Far forced himself to be patient with his parents' pace. It took a couple extra days to get there, but he was glad to be on the way.

When they finally made it to the Onondaga village, the first person they saw was Trillium. She had spent every moment she could with her eyes on the path, looking at that spot where she had last seen Wanders Far. It had been several months, but she clearly remembered Wanders Far told her he would be on his way back the moment the snow melted.

Bear Fat watched as her youngest son wrapped his arms around the pretty young girl who ran up the path to meet him. She took Big Canoe's hand in her own, looked quickly in her husband's eyes, raised both of her eyebrows, and a bittersweet, salty tear rolled down her check. She was proud.

A few minutes later, Wanders Far introduced Trillium to his parents. They made their way down the path, stood briefly at the shore of the lake and then Trillium led them into the Onondaga village. She took them on a tour, introduced them to many people, and answered a few questions. Bear Fat and Big Canoe had never seen such a large village. In fact they had never seen one even half its size.

They were warmly received in Trillium's longhouse by her mother Owl, and her aunt, Cattail. They were just beginning to prepare dinner. Bear Fat offered gifts from her basket that became part of dinner for everyone in the longhouse.

Bright Star and Snapping Turtle arrived first. Snapping Turtle was an outgoing man who liked to tell jokes and funny little stories, and Bright Star liked to be the subject of the stories as often as possible. She interjected frequently.

New Face came forward from her compartment at the back of the longhouse and was thrilled to meet Bear Fat. There was a lot she hoped to learn from the woman who had presided over a counsel and served as matriarch for so long.

They had finished dinner and were gathered together at the hearth when Justice arrived. She had had a busy day tending to the small children in the village, then she had to help a family who was welcoming the arrival of a new baby.

Bear Fat was talking to New Face when her eyes met Justice's eyes. She stopped talking in the middle of a sentence. She caught a chill, and she shuddered. There was something about that girl. Bear Fat couldn't explain what it was, and she couldn't stop staring at her, rude as it was. Strangely, the young girl did not look away. Finally, Bear Fat looked back at New Face, and apologized for losing track of her thoughts.

When Justice was introduced to Bear Fat, the older woman said, "I'm sorry. I didn't mean to stare. I feel like I know you. Have we met before?" They talked for a while, easily and comfortably, as if they had known each other for years.

Then a visitor arrived at the door. Seeks Wampum had heard that Wanders Far had arrived in the village. They greeted each other like brothers, hand to elbow, elbow to hand. He offered to tell some stories, since there was a group assembled. Seeks Wampum always loved to have an audience. He searched his brain quickly for just the right one while they got comfortable.

Everyone found a warm spot around the central fire, and Seeks Wampum positioned himself so that everyone could see him. He put his hands on his hips, legs spread slightly apart, puffed his chest forward, shoulders back, and he was in character. He took a deep breath, and just before he uttered his first syllable, Bear Fat shrieked.

Bear Fat sat there, all eyes upon her, with her hand over her mouth pointing at Justice's foot. There was a blackberry shaped birthmark on her ankle. She was sitting next to her long-lost daughter. The public composure required by her position didn't concern Bear Fat. At that moment she burst into tears, covering her sobbing face with both hands, head between her knees. Big Canoe tried to console her, reaching his arm across her back, placing his hand on her shoulder.

She sat up, trying to regain her composure. Her confused face laughed and cried at the same time. Bear Fat said, "Please forgive me. It's just that a long time ago I had a baby girl with a birth mark just exactly like the one Justice has on her ankle. I was digging for roots in the woods a short distance away, when someone came along and swooped my baby girl up, and she has been gone ever since. Not one day has gone by that I haven't thought about my lost baby girl. Not one day."

Justice had instinctively covered her birthmark with her hand the moment Bear Fat started screaming and pointing. When Bear Fat finished speaking, Justice looked at her mother, who had tears in her eyes. She looked back and forth between the two women. Nobody had ever told her that she had been adopted. Justice gripped her ankle, as if to keep her birthmark to herself. She felt the heavy weight of being the center of attention, and she froze. She didn't know whether to be happy or sad. She wished she was alone, anywhere. She had a lot to contemplate.

Cattail stood up and said, "It's a miracle. To think after all of these years you have found your baby girl, here in our village. Many years ago, a Huron man was passing through the woods carrying a baby, but otherwise alone, very far from his home. Our men captured him in the woods. He was tortured, and he eventually died. Me and my husband waited years for a baby to come to us, and one never did, so we took the Huron baby and raised her as our own. Justice was the answer to my prayers. I got to be the mother I always wanted to be. Now she is the answer to two mothers' dreams tonight." Tears streamed down Justice's face. Her mother's words helped her see the shocking news as a wonderful gift.

Bear Fat turned to Big Canoe and whispered, "We found her." Then she stood and embraced Cattail. "Thank you for being a wonderful mother for our baby girl. I am so grateful."

Seeks Wampum quickly stood up and concluded, "The end."

The marriage negotiations were easy. Bear Fat and Owl planned a quick wedding on the shores of the lake just outside the village at sunrise, three days later. The men set out in search of big game for a feast, and the women prepared the rest of the details. Three days later, Wanders Far and Trillium were married. Friends and family wished them well, and they were about to set off alone on a wedding trip as husband and wife.

At that moment, Entangled raged upon the scene. New Face jumped to intercept him. He was threatening to abolish the alliance unless all tribes, clans, and villages were represented in the village immediately. Winter had released its hold, and it was time to find an enemy to engage. New Face assured him that they would start to gather delegates at once. Placated somewhat, Entangled stormed off to make plans for summer sorties.

New Face said, "I am devastated to have to ask you, today of all days. You're the best runner we have and the only one I can count on at this moment. I need you to gather representatives from all the tribes as fast as possible."

Wanders Far had no choice but to answer his calling. The family made quick arrangements. Trillium would join Bear Fat and Big Canoe at Copperas Pond and Wanders Far would meet them there as soon as he completed his run, from west to east across the lands of the unified tribes. Then Wanders Far could head north to Copperas Pond.

Trillium and Wanders Far spent ten minutes alone together, where the trail entered the woods on the path toward the west. There was no choice. Anyone who spent time in Entangled's village knew that lives could be saved by preventing Entangled's murderous rages.

The next morning, Trillium set out with Bear Fat and Big Canoe. They got to know each other better on the way to Garoga Creek, where they spent two days before heading north with Squash, Blue Arrow, and Squash's children. Somersault was delighted to meet Wanders Far's flower wife, and they became kindred spirits.

Wanders Far dutifully ran the required route and summoned all the representatives necessary to attend Entangled's war council meeting. He felt like he had been yearning forever. At last he had married the girl of his dreams, only to be sent away before spending even one night together.

Weeks later, when all of the delegates were finally assembled, the council began. Wanders Far sat in the back, out of sight. Entangled sat on a big chair on a pedestal. New Face stood at his side and delegates from all the tribes surrounded them. Entangled made the case for war against the Hurons. In a summer campaign, unlike any before, he dreamed of total annihilation of the enemy. The leaders of the other tribes weren't convinced. The enemy wasn't rich enough to make it worth their while. The cost of achieving the objective seemed high. The debate went on for hours.

Entangled became enraged. He had understood the promise made by New Face to be all the tribes would worship him as their supreme ruler.

New Face knew Entangled well enough to know what would happen if he wasn't placated in some way, but she couldn't think of a way to give him enough of what he wanted. The leaders of the other tribes were becoming more stubborn. She could see it in his eyes—clearly Entangled wanted to rip her face off, or maybe something even worse than that.

When the council meeting began, Wanders Far closed his eyes. He sat cross-legged, his hands wrapped around the magic crystal talisman at his neck. He concentrated harder than he ever had in his life. He had always known Spirit to show up when it should.

Finally, when it felt like his veins would burst from the pressure, his spirit penetrated the thick walls of Entangled's soul. It was as dark as the back of a cave. It was as noisy as a raucous band of Entangled's warriors, plus a loud thumping drumbeat. It was as thick as the black muck at the bottom of a shallow swamp. Wanders Far's presence glowed amongst the gloom.

For many weeks along the trail, Wanders Far had planned for that day.

He visualized rolling in the thick mud to conceal his presence. Then he moved quickly and quietly to survey the territory. All of the energy was engaged in an angry display, collecting itself for a physical outburst. Though angry, that energy was excited at the same time. Violence was almost at hand. The energy relished the opportunity to manifest. They had been held at bay since the previous year's military campaigns. It was a combustible situation.

Wanders Far saw the dark spirit, cloaked in shadow. He noticed the eagle on one shoulder and the hawk on the other. He felt as if they were looking for him among the crowd of arguing council members. It was Wanders Far they feared. They were unaware of Wanders Far's presence in Entangled's soul. Wanders Far aimed to keep it that way.

Wanders Far thought of a black snake and visualized his body slithering past all the angry energy, swimming through the mud just by moving his shoulders.

Entangled rose from his throne, muscles flexed, weapons at

hand. He felt like biting something with his molars. The grip of his hand on the wooden axe handle almost burst it into splinters.

It was hot when Wanders Far found the center of Entangled's brain. Wanders Far's physical body sweated profusely, sitting there quietly in his robe, not that anyone was paying attention to him.

A massive force of adrenaline shot through Wanders Far. He liberated his pent-up warrior spirit. He unleashed a blood curdling ferocious scream from both his physical and spiritual forms. He had gone undetected. The dark spirit had missed his presence. Alerted by the scream, the dark spirit moved fast. It got to the core in a flash, yet just an instant too slowly. Wanders Far thrust his magic crystal talisman into the core of Entangled's cerebellum, which triggered a massive explosion in Entangled's brain. It was a massive aneurism.

Immediately he returned to the form of the black snake. He slithered as fast as he could. He didn't have long. He had to return to the entry point. The hawk, the eagle, and the dark spirit were in fast pursuit. They knew where he was going even if they couldn't see him beneath the mud.

Entangled's physical form collapsed just inches from contact with New Face. Her cranium had been moments away from being split by an axe. She stood there, stunned. Though she lived in the face of danger as She Who Lives Along the Road to War, she didn't know how to react at that moment where she almost died at Entangled's hand. His body continued to thrash and squirm on the ground at her feet. Suddenly she noticed another commotion in the lodge. At the back of the room someone else was flopping around on the floor. She ran to see what was happening there, happy to be moving away from Entangled.

Her jaw dropped, astonished to see Wanders Far, naked, sweaty, bright red, and glowing, writhing around like a snake. His eyes were rolled up into his lids, so only the whites were visible. Then there was a bright white flash. Wanders Far's spirit returned to his body.

He stretched his arms wide. His skin, red and enflamed, began to re-turn to its normal color. He was breathing heavily but as his system calmed down, his breathing returned to normal. The muscles in his face began to relax.

Chapter Twenty-Two
The First Full Moon of Summer

Wanders Far rested one day before returning to the trail. Entangled was dead. The tribe was officially in mourning. As he made his final preparations to leave, it occurred to Wanders Far that the grieving tribe looked jubilant and festive. When he and Trillium returned in the fall there would be a new chief. He didn't care who they chose. They would no longer have to follow Entangled.

For half a day, Wanders Far thought about his own role in Entangled's demise. He had never killed a man before. He hoped he would never kill a man again. Too weak to ever challenge Entangled in the physical world, Wanders Far had found a way to defeat him in the spirit world. In the end it was all the same. He could hardly disown his role. He had planned it for weeks. He visualized every detail he could imagine. He thought of every possible scenario he could consider. Someone should have done it years sooner. Entangled would never have suspected that he could be brought down by a scrawny messenger that played with toddlers. Wanders Far knew he had saved countless lives by ending the life of Entangled. He would have done it even if he didn't have to defend New Face. He thought of his friend Seeks Wampum, and the wife and children Entangled had murdered before his eyes. He thought of Two Rivers' mother who Entangled had clubbed to death, many years before. Avenged.

He resolved never to mention the evil chief's name again. For the rest of his trip his thoughts were of the future, waiting for him in the mountains.

He finally arrived at Copperas Pond just as spring was giving way to summer. It was the middle of the morning when he ran into the little clearing where Trillium and Bear Fat were working on curing skins. Trillium dropped her work, ran and jumped into Wander's Far's arms. A couple of minutes later, Wander's Far asked Trillium, "How fast can you pack for a couple days away?"

Wanders Far filled his pack with thick warm bearskins and Bear Fat gave him some food for their journey. They were on their way in less than fifteen minutes. Trillium didn't even know where they were going. She hardly cared.

They hiked for hours. The going was steep. They talked the whole way. Each had so much to share with the other. Finally, they were alone together. Wanders Far constructed a bearskin enclosure under the rock where he took cover during the storm that came on the third day of his quest on the mountain. He wanted to be prepared. He knew the weather on the mountain could be bad. It wasn't necessary.

There was no wind. There was hardly even a breeze. The air was unseasonably warm, even without cloud cover. There were only the slightest puffs of clouds that occasionally drifted across the well-lit night sky. The moon was full and shone brightly, illuminating the boulders on the top of the mountain. It seemed like night and day at the same time.

The couple embraced tentatively. They kissed, tenderly at first and then with increasing urgency. Wanders Far whispered, "Tonight there is no chance of being interrupted by Justice, and there is no chance of being sent away by New Face!" A few minutes later they were on the bearskin blanket. Given all the longing that preceded it, it only took a few minutes to consecrate their union.

They lay naked together between the bearskins on the top of the mountain for a couple of hours, talking quietly, caressing gently and intimately. There was no longing. They were exactly where they wanted to be and living in a moment that they wished could last forever.

When the moon reached its zenith, they made love a second time. Afterwards, he kissed each of her closed eyelids and said in a quiet low voice, "The Great Spirit must be pleased with us to give us such a gift." They drifted off to sleep for a couple of hours, then they watched the sun rise from the top of the mountain.

The second day was warmer still. They didn't bother with clothes. They spent most of the day basking in the sunshine, enjoying each other as man and wife.

On the third day, they hiked back down the mountain. Before they started down, Wanders Far suggested, "How about if we come back here and do this again, the first full moon of summer, every year?"

Trillium wrapped her arms around his waist, gave him a kiss, and nodded.

They spent the rest of the summer in a small wickiup they constructed on Copperas Pond, across the pond from Bear Fat, Big Canoe, and Squash's family. They were inseparable, and fortunate to have so much time alone together before the reality of hard work, toil, and survival reentered their lives at the end of the summer.

The following spring, in the Onondaga village, Trillium gave birth to twin baby boys as the last of the snow was melting from the trails. Wanders Far had warned her to have two of everything ready. She was astonished that he could know what she did not. Having one baby was challenging enough, but to have two on the same day was a rare occurrence. A month later they set out for their summer residence. Each of them carried one of the babies as well as their pack baskets.

Wanders Far and Trillium arrived at Copperas Pond in time for the first full moon of summer. Bear Fat and Big Canoe were pleased to learn they were grandparents again, and happy to see Wanders Far and Trillium after the long fall, winter, and spring. After a couple of days, Wanders Far and Trillium prepared the packs and the papooses for a trip up the mountain. After they had left the pond, Big Canoe asked Bear Fat, "Why would you take babies to the top of a mountain?"

Bear Fat laughed, and said, "Well, why wouldn't you?"

In the years that followed, Wanders Far, Trillium, and their growing family set out each summer for Copperas Pond at the foot of Whiteface Mountain. Wanders Far's children and generations of his ancestors heard the story of how the mountain got its white face and were honored to know that magic was part of their heritage. As the legend concluded: "Those who see with the eyes of romance can distinguish in the mountain mists the form of the great white stag standing alert on a rocky ledge just below the white face of the mountain."

Chapter Twenty-Three
A Young Man with an Old Soul

Every summer for fifty years, Wanders Far and Trillium hiked up Whiteface Mountain to celebrate their wedding anniversary.

It was a perfect afternoon. They took their time ascending the mountain, stopping for lots of breaks, and to enjoy the trip along the way.

They talked about many subjects. They talked about their children. Wanders Far and Trillium had three sets of identical twins. The oldest pair were the sons they conceived on the top of the mountain. A few years later came a pair of daughters. Then they had a second set of daughters. They talked about their numerous grandchildren, and then they talked about their many great-grandchildren. One of those favored Wanders Far and followed in his footsteps, quite literally. The small boy was always at Wanders Far's feet and came to be known as Shadow.

Trillium teased her husband about dragging his poor old mother up to the mountains. Wanders Far said, "She wants to die at Copperas Pond, so she insisted that we bring her." Bear Fat was 101-years-old that summer, astonishing considering many of the people were lucky to live half that long. She maintained her faculties, her memories, and she could walk at a fair pace. Long ago she had relinquished her duties as matriarch, leaving her people in the excellent care of her granddaughter, Somersault. Wanders Far continued, "I don't know how I know this, but she will not die this summer. She is blessed with the gift of longevity." Wanders Far was happy to talk about Bear Fat at that moment. He and his mother had always shared a powerfully strong bond.

The old couple stopped to rest near the weathered remains of the small hut that Wanders Far and Follows Stars built for Wanders Far's rite of passage so many years before. The fire pit remained, and a log bench in front of the fire was well-preserved.

Trillium never tired of hearing about her husband's visions. She didn't ask often, and she hadn't heard the story in many years. On that early summer's afternoon, she asked her husband to tell her again about what he saw when he spent three days and nights on the mountain when he was 15-years-old.

Wanders Far shared a warm look with his beloved wife, as if to say, "Thanks for asking." He enjoyed remembering and reflecting on his time with Follows Stars and the momentous milestone when he became a man.

Wanders Far held Trillium's hand as the fire crackled and spit from the sappy joints of the pine twigs they had used for fuel. He spoke slowly and reverently about Follows Stars and the great white stag. He recalled the strange visions of the future, filled with people he couldn't comprehend, describing them the best that he could. He smiled and teased his wife about the vision of her sister, Bright Star, the Moon Girl of his dreams who had come to him from above on the top of the mountain so many years before.

Trillium interrupted, "You don't know it all. You wise old seer! You couldn't even tell one sister from another." Trillium winked at Wanders Far, a familiar exchange between the pair, then she tilted her head and rested it on his shoulder.

Wanders Far continued, "It has been an amazing journey. I only wanted to hike the trails, run the ridges, and see the world.

It wasn't my choice to see into souls, spirits, and the future, but I haven't minded following the path I was meant to follow. Often I am amazed when the reality of a vision is far more glorious than it appeared when I saw it in my dreams."

"Like your Moon Girl vision," Trillium laughed. "You know, we were meant to be together, you and me, Wanders Far," she added, tenderly.

He looked into her eyes, and said, "I have never told you that part of the story before. I have never told anyone those words spoken by Moon Girl. Not even Follows Stars. I wasn't allowed to. What took you so long? Now I know for sure I haven't spent the last fifty years with the wrong girl," he joked.

Trillium shook her head back and forth and said, as if informing an audience, "Long ago I married a young man with an old soul, and a gift so powerful he can't tell whether he was right until fifty years later!"

Wanders far graciously laughed at himself. With his index finger, he brushed a wisp of hair from her cheek and tucked it behind her ear. They shared a quick kiss. In a serious voice, Wanders Far said, "The Great Spirit shows me what the Great Spirit wants me to see and doesn't always tell me how to see it."

He stretched his strong legs toward the fire, warming the bottoms of his feet. His wife could tell that he was beginning to have a vision. In a low, deep, stoic voice, Wanders Far revealed, "There will be another young man with an old soul, a long, long time from now. He will sit in this spot. He will live in the shadow of the giant mountain all of the days of his life. He will know great sadness. He will also know great joy. I picture him wearing hard leather shoes, with shiny knives strapped to the bottom, and he is twirling around on ice. His movement is fast and daring, and yet his movement is also graceful and poetic. I also see him at Copperas Pond. He is younger there. He is happy. I see him jumping from the ledge."

Wanders Far grew quiet for a moment. Tears sprang to the corners of his eyes. Then they began to stream down his face. He looked into the eyes of his wife. "I see he has found Grandmother's lost necklace. She will be so pleased."

He turned his head sideways, like a confused puppy. "I see this boy is a man. An older man. He is looking at a magic box that is telling him that he is connected to us. This magic can tell him that we are a part of him. He did not know this. He is pleased to learn that he has the blood of the people within him. He is closing his eyes. He is having his own vision. He sees me on my journey to the Great Roaring Waterfalls. He sees me with Follows Stars on Whiteface Mountain."

Suddenly, Wanders Far's entire body was covered with goosebumps. He looked at his wife, awestruck.

"He is me."

CPSIA information can be obtained
at www.ICGtesting.com
Printed in the USA
LVHW090713121119
637080LV00003B/289/P